Send Me Down a Miracle

Han Nolan

Harcourt Brace & Company

San Diego   New York   London

Requests for permission to make copies of any part
of the work should be mailed to:
Permissions Department, Harcourt Brace & Company,
6277 Sea Harbor Drive, Orlando, Florida 32887-6777.

Scripture quotations taken from the *Holy Bible, New
International Version.* Copyright © 1973, 1978, 1984
by International Bible Society. Used by permission of
Zondervan Publishing House.

Library of Congress Cataloging-in-Publication Data
Nolan, Han.
Send me down a miracle/Han Nolan.—1st ed.
p.   cm.
Summary: A sleepy, God-fearing southern town
erupts in chaos when a flamboyant artist from New
York City returns to her birthplace for an artistic
experiment.
ISBN 0-15-200979-5
ISBN 0-15-200978-7 (pbk.)
[1. Artists—Fiction.   2. Christian life—Fiction.]
I. Title.
PZ7.N6783Se   1996
[Fic]—dc20   95–38169

Text was set in Meridien
Designed by Lydia D'moch
Printed in the United States of America

C D E F
D E F (pbk.)

For Brian—always

And in loving memory of my aunt,
Helen B. Newton

1

I was fourteen the summer Mama took off for the Birdcage Collectors' Convention and we had ourselves what is now known in this town as the Adrienne Dabney Incident.

'Course the only reason Adrienne was blamed for everything was because she was a stranger in town and a New York artist to boot!

Sharalee Marshall's mama said that Adrienne had no need taking the huff the way she did 'cause a body wasn't anybody around here 'less they'd had an incident named after them, and really, if this town had any sense atall, we would have named it after my daddy, especially him being the preacher and all, and we should forgive him for his disgrace.

I know it was on everyone's mind to call it another Mad Joe Dunn Incident, but no one was talking about that. That part of the story's been erased, forgotten, a skeleton in this town's closet no one dares to bring out, except for me, right now. See, I got to, 'cause I know I was the one who started it all. I was the one who loved her.

The moment I saw Adrienne Dabney flop down in Mama's old wingback chair and prop her bare feet up on Mama's inlaid mother-of-pearl coffee table, I knew I was in love.

She arrived in town in the middle of June, the same day Mama took off, and law, it was the hottest, driest June anyone could remember. Already the grass had turned to straw under the scorching sun, and when we rode down the dirt roads on our bikes the red dust would rise like smoke clouds and we'd choke on it and our throats would burn like we were riding with the sun in our mouths. Then in walked Adrienne, into our tidy home, looking like some wild jungle woman with fat, frizzed-out hair, rings on her toes, and this long, brightly colored skirt that was practically see-through. She was saying words like "creativity" and "stupendous" and "artistic merit," and it was like I'd found myself in a cool summer shower dancing and laughing and throwing my head back to catch the raindrops in my mouth. And every word she said, every gesture she made was like more rain washing over me, waking me up to something—something exciting and dangerous, but I didn't know what, I just knew I wanted it. But Daddy sure didn't.

Adrienne pushed aside one of Mama's birdcages with her bare foot and I saw Daddy's eyes move from the sandals kicked off beneath the old wingback to Adrienne slunk down in the chair so her legs could stretch to the inlaid mother-of-pearl, and then up to her hair, all long and frizzed-out with strands of silver running through it, and I swanee, I could see a shudder travel down Daddy's back and settle in his hiney like the woman had slipped a frozen anchovy down his shirt.

She said she loved my name. She tried it out a few times: "Charity, Charity," like she was tasting fine wine, and then she said it was splendid, a splendid name, and I thought to myself that never did a word sound so fine as "splendid."

My eight-year-old sister, Grace, kept drifting in and out of the room like a fairy unable to light on her lily pad, and Adrienne just took it for normal. And maybe where she came from it was.

She said she and her lover (her lover!) had been in Paris because she had an art show there and did we know Montmartre and had we been to the Louvre, which she pronounced with lots of spit and throat-clearing sounds, just like a real French person. Of course we didn't know anything about Paris, but Daddy tried to say something about it anyway and then gave up halfway through, expecting Mama to come to his rescue the way she always did, forgetting that Mama was already two weeks gone.

"Ah," Adrienne said, "you must go. Everyone should go at least once in their lives. La Tour Eiffel, Chartres, l'Arc de Triomphe—oh, and if you're into people watching, the sidewalk cafés are marvelous. I sat there for hours every day, sketching, painting. The colors are brilliant. The people are fantastic; so interesting. You know the French hold their mouths differently. Like this." She drew her lips forward, puckering and pouting at the same time. "It's amazing! My God! I've got to go back there."

She did. She said, "My God," right in front of Daddy, and then on top of it, something else about her lover and "ooh-la-la," right there in our living room, and didn't stop to catch her breath or check to see if what she said was upsetting anybody or anything. She just slouched back in that wingback, dangled her hand over the armrest, and twirled the stem of her sunglasses round and round in her hands, and went right on talking and saying whatever she pleased. And I knew, soon as I got up to my room, I was going to pull out my sunglasses and practice twirling and slouching in front of my mirror till I looked just like her.

She told us about the types of cheeses they had in Paris, with names that sounded nothing like Swiss or cheddar or American, and then about Degas and Rodin, which I thought were more cheese names but turned out to be famous artists like her, only dead.

She told us about her art, how she paints landscapes and cityscapes and shapes and such in oils and watercolors. And we knew some about that 'cause she was born right here in Casper and even though she did move away when she was still a baby, she'd been written up in our paper. It was all about how famous she had become and what kind of painting she did and such. We kept the article tacked to our bulletin board in the back of the church till it got so dry and yellow it just crumbled into pieces, but we still had the tack up there, in memory of it, I guess.

After so much art talk and Adrienne slouching in Mama's chair half the day, Daddy was ready for her to leave. He stood up and then so did I, and Grace was already standing, on her way out the door again, but Adrienne didn't move. She said she'd come over for a purpose.

She said, "I'm very distressed by all the attention I've been getting down here." She set her sunglasses on top of her head and reached for a candy mint without even asking. She popped it in her mouth and leaned back in her chair. Daddy sat back down on the camel-back sofa all stiff and bristly, patting down his hairpiece, and I just stood there watching like this was some exciting new TV show.

"Really, I can't have it," Adrienne said. "I'm working on an important project, an experiment, and I can't have your people coming over, dropping off food, and wanting to chat for hours on end."

Daddy tugged at his shirt collar, and I could see his face was blotching up red hot. I stepped forward and offered her another mint.

"Thank you, Charity," she said to me. Just

so fine. "Thank you, Charity." I can still hear her voice and remember how it sounded, like a slip of ice melting down the throat. I sat back down and said it to myself, "Thank you, Charity," and then I caught sight of Daddy looking sour at me and decided to save it for nighttime when I was alone in my room.

"Miss Dabney," Daddy said, straining with politeness, "surely you must be able to understand that this is not New York City. We're a small town and your arrival is big news. Everyone knows everyone around here, and when a stranger comes to town it's only polite that our congregation welcome her."

Adrienne laughed. "Small town is right. I never realized. My mother used to tell me stories about growing up here, about the old Dabney homestead and how it would someday be mine. What I never realized was that the few people she used to talk about were probably the only people in town. No wonder I couldn't find it on the map—my God, this is a small town."

"It sure is," I said, hoping Adrienne would stop taking the Lord's name in vain before Daddy popped a blood vessel. "Why, it's so small you can hold it in the palm of your hand without fear of spilling."

She laughed and nodded and said to me,

"Charity, I think I'm going to like you." And I felt the thrill of those words right down to my toes, which I had been imagining with a couple of silver rings on them like hers; but then Daddy cleared his throat and started talking again and those rings just popped right off my feet.

"I'm sorry we've been bothering you with our visits. It was certainly not our intention. You can rest assured that I'll have my congregation—"

"Look," Adrienne interrupted. "It's just that I came here to work, and when some ancient woman rolls her car down my driveway and honks her horn outside my window until I come out—well, I can't have it."

"That would be Miss Tuney Mae Jenkins," I said.

Adrienne nodded and her sunglasses slipped off her head onto her nose. She left them there.

"Yes, I went outside to see what all the honking was for and she threw open her door and yelled to me, 'Hey, sugar, come get me out of this contraption.' *Hey, sugar!* My God! And then she goes up my stairs and into my house as if it's hers, turning on the lights and putting some godawful dessert into the fridge.

Well, you know, you saw it, Reverend Pitt-man, when you stopped by."

What Adrienne didn't know was that the whole town knew about Daddy's visit. What with him being the preacher of the only church in town, it was his business and his duty to welcome Miss Adrienne. So he trotted on over to her place with a peanut pie he had me make using Mama's recipe, and law if she didn't refuse to invite him in, just kept him out on the stoop and told him how she hated peanuts, thought they carried worms, so no use her keeping the pie. Then she dug Miss Tuney Mae's pecan deluxe out of her fridge and shoved it off on Daddy, saying how she feels the same way about pecans. Imagine coming to Casper, Alabama, where all we grow is peanuts and pecans and tobacco and such, and her not liking any of it.

When Miss Tuney Mae found out Adrienne palmed off her pecan deluxe on Daddy, she had plenty to say about it, *and* her. I heard her talking to Old Higgs after church, telling him how Adrienne still had all her furniture covered in sheets.

"Didn't pull a one of 'em off, not even to offer me a seat," she said. "And, mercy, it was dark in there. Now, I offered to send the

Dooley brothers over to pry the boards off her winders, and know what she said? Said she wanted them left on. Said she didn't need help cleaning, neither, and just looking around at all the dust and her artsy stuff piled up high in the shadows told me she was needing lots of help, but she said she planned to leave it exactly the way it was for a while. Now, imagine that, would you. Leaving it like no one was living there. Like she wasn't a live soul breathing in there."

Folks were calling the way she was living spooky and bizarre and thinking she was maybe one of those modern-day witches or something. And hearing all this got me just dying to go over and meet her, but Daddy told me to stay away till he found out which way the wind blew with "that peculiar artist woman," as he called her.

I knew if Mama were still home she would have gone over to that house and found out all there was to know about Miss Adrienne Dabney. That's what Mama was good at, getting people to tell their stories, and she didn't go spreading them all over town like Miss Tuney Mae, either.

I tried to do as Daddy said and stay away, but I couldn't help passing by her house occasionally 'cause it was practically on the way to everywhere, it being on the main road and all. So me and my best friend, Sharalee, would just happen to ride by the Dabney place on our bikes every once in a while and there it was, same as always, boarded up and leaning to the right, with the paint peeling, looking like some forgotten old man, but we knew she was in there walking around in all that dark, full of all kinds of mystery and intrigue.

Then there she was sitting in our living room, in Mama's chair, and Mama two weeks gone and missing all the excitement.

Daddy's voice jumped into my thoughts. "Just what exactly is this experiment you were talking about?" he asked Adrienne.

"Ah, my sensory deprivation project." Adrienne shoved her glasses back on top of her head and sat forward in the chair. "You see, I plan to lock myself in my house for a month, living in the dark, not seeing or hearing or doing anything except meditating. For my art, you understand. To give my eyes and my mind a rest. And then when I come out, well, I hope to have some kind of rebirth experience. Seeing with new eyes. Creating new art, fresh." She nodded at me. "Like your daughter here. She's a breath of fresh air. I want everything to seem that way. I want my paintings to be that way."

I couldn't keep from grinning, half-silly, I was so pleased with what she said. Imagine me being a breath of fresh air! Wouldn't Sharalee have something to say when I told her that.

Daddy said, "You plan to lock yourself in your house?"

"That's right," Adrienne said.

"For a month?"

"Yes, for a month."

"No, I'm afraid you can't do that. No, it won't do. We can't have that here. No." Daddy stood up. "I'm afraid that's impossible. Anything could happen in that old place. Why, you don't even have a phone in there! No, I just couldn't be held responsible for any—"

"Oh, of course not. I wouldn't ask you to." Adrienne stood up, too, and then so did I. Grace was just wandering back in, so she was already standing.

"No, I was hoping you could just tell all your people to hold off on their welcome a month or so, that's all. The rest, of course, is up to me."

"No, I don't like it." Daddy shook his head.

"I'm not asking you to like it. I'm not *asking* you at all. I certainly don't need your permission to live as I choose in my own house."

Daddy scowled. "We don't take to strange doings around here, Miss Dabney. Now, I know you and your artist friends do all kinds of—of peculiar things in that New York City, but you're in Casper now and I can tell you we don't like this sort of thing. No indeed. We're a quiet, God-fearing town and—"

"Reverend Pittman, just what kinds of things do you imagine going on in a boarded-up house when I'm by myself?"

"Well now, I know anything can pass for normal in New York City, but down here, well, this kind of business is just insane. Yes, that's just what it is, insane. Now, meditating on the Lord, praying, and being reborn are all fine things, and we have a wonderful church—"

"I'm afraid you don't understand," Adrienne interrupted. "I won't be meditating on the Lord, Reverend Pittman, and I don't believe in prayer."

"Nonsense! Of course you believe in prayer!" Daddy's face was red, and sweat was running out from under his hairpiece. "What is this world coming to when a woman even considers sitting in the dark in a locked-up, boarded-up house, with no God to guide her? Only evil can be contemplated in such a circumstance." He turned to me and Grace. "The devil is in our very midst."

He sounded as if he were about to launch into one of his sermons, but Adrienne cut him off, asking me, "Charity, what do you think?"

I blinked at her, and I know my face was red 'cause there she was, looking at me with this knowing kind of look. Maybe she had seen the excitement in my face or eyes or something. I could tell she knew I thought it was thrilling. I thought *she* was thrilling. Listening to her and watching her was as new and exciting as finding snow in my pockets, and I wanted to say so; but see, Daddy knew about these things. He knew without a single doubt what was the devil's work and what wasn't; and thinking on it a second, it seemed way too exciting to be anything but a devil's temptation. I shook my head and started to speak, and Daddy jumped in.

"I'm not interested in a child's opinion of the situation. Nor should you be. I don't take to people using children that way, nor to people who use art as an excuse to act crazy and do any of the devil's work they please. This is a quiet town with good, decent people in it. I think you will find you've made a great mistake coming here. Now I think you should be on your way."

Daddy stormed out of the room, and we followed him to the front door. Adrienne kept talking, saying how this was all ridiculous and how she was not there to cause trouble but to live quietly, undisturbed, for a month or so. Daddy wasn't listening. I could tell 'cause he was jingling the change in his pocket the same way he did anytime someone tried to say something he didn't want to hear. He opened the front door, and we heard the sound of gunshots blasting. Daddy stepped outside and stood there jingling his change as fast as he could, waiting for Adrienne to leave.

Adrienne stood in the doorway and looked out to the end of the driveway. "What is that man doing out there? What's going on?"

We were so used to old Mad Joe, we hadn't given him a thought. I watched as he took aim and fired another shot into the road. "Oh, don't worry," I said. "That's just Mad Joe. He likes to shoot worm bellies. 'Course, it being so dry this spring, it's probably just ants or something."

Adrienne nodded. "Ah yes, a quiet, God-fearing town."

2

I had to wait a whole week before I got to tell Sharalee about Adrienne, what with Sharalee's new job at the Food World and all. We had planned to meet in the barn back of the Marshalls' house, only Sharalee was still eating dinner when I got there, so I had to wait out in the barn by myself for her to finish up. I had taken the shortcut, stepping through the hole in the back some cow once made and then got her head stuck in.

I looked around and shivered. The barn was all shadows, and empty except for the coffins. Mr. Marshall makes coffins—just the

shells, not the satin and brass accessories—
and stores them in the barn. They were lined
up so straight and still, every one of them ooz-
ing out death like a leak of black oil. I couldn't
keep from looking at them, watching them,
thinking any minute one of the lids might
start to creak open. I tried not to think about
it. I busied myself by setting out the food I had
brought over, which I always had to do 'cause
Sharalee's mama had Sharalee on a diet and
wouldn't let her have anything with flavor.
Then finally I heard Sharalee's kitchen door
slam and her flip-flops slapping at the dirt, and
I relaxed and watched for her to step through
the hole.

"Hey, girl," she called out, walking toward
me and yanking down on her T-shirt. "What
kind of dessert you bring me?"

"Nothing much, just some hush puppies
left over from dinner."

Sharalee looked them over and gave them
a sniff like some old coon dog. "Well, who
made them, you or your mama?"

"I did. Mama's gone off to that birdcage
convention, remember?"

"She's still gone? I thought that only
lasted a week." Sharalee popped a hush puppy
in her mouth. "Don't it last just a week?"

17

"Yes, but she's gone visiting and such. She's gone to Tennessee," I said, repeating what I had said to just about every nosy-body in town.

Sharalee popped another hush puppy in her mouth, even though she wasn't through chewing down the first one. She shook her head. "Weird," she said.

"What's weird?"

She shrugged and licked the grease off her fingers. "Your mama. It's like she puts all her living into one week of convention and the rest of the year she's just—well, kind of—you know."

"No, I don't know, and anyway, what a thing to say!"

"Well, it's not me that's saying it. I heard Miss Tuney Mae Jenkins telling my mama that what your mama needs is more frequent hydration."

"So what is that supposed to mean?"

Sharalee shrugged like what she was about to say didn't mean anything, but I could tell by the gleam in her eyes that she was getting ready to say something cutting.

"It's like she's a prune all year, you know, all dried up, and then come springtime and the convention she turns into a plum. Least that's how Miss Tuney Mae put it." She popped the last hush puppy in her mouth.

"Well, what does she know?" I said, trying to push away the memory I had of Mama the day she left. I could still see her dressed in all that green. Green pants and a green-and-white fern-leaf shirt and a straw sun hat dyed a bright shiny green. Law, if she didn't look just like a parrot escaped from one of her cages. And Daddy was fit to be tied 'cause he said green was way too tacky for a preacher's wife to be running around in. But Mama wore it anyway, so Daddy refused to kiss her good-bye or wave or anything, forgetting, I guess, that Mama and Aunt Nooney were going on to Tennessee to stay with Maggie and them after the convention.

There was no telling how long they'd be away. That's what Mama told me. And the way she said it, tossing it out, carefree-like, and not looking at me when she said it, was strange, not like Mama atall. And I remember her squeezing me and Grace real tight when she hugged us good-bye. Squeezing like she wanted our imprints on her body 'cause the hugs were going to have to last such a long time. Then she got in the car and she and Aunt Nooney rolled out of the drive, their car loaded down with the birdcages they were hoping to trade at the convention. Me and Grace stood on the porch waving at the back of their car, and Mama was waving, too, only she wasn't looking back. I remember that; she never looked back.

I scowled at Sharalee with my hands on my hips. "I've been waiting all week to talk to you and there you are going on about Mama."

"So what? You haven't asked me about my bagging job at the Food World and it's my first week." Sharalee lifted the lid of a coffin and pulled out a bag of chocolate chip cookies. "I'm thinking that maybe the reason you haven't even bothered to call me this week is 'cause you're jealous of my real job in Dothan while you're stuck here in Casper with the farmers and young'uns teaching Vacation Bible School for your daddy."

"I am not jealous. It's just that what I got to tell you I couldn't say over the phone."

Sharalee moved in closer. "Oh? You keeping secrets from your daddy?"

"It's no secret. It's just—Oh, Sharalee! I met her! I saw her and spoke to her. I even went over to her house before she shut herself in for good. She's wonderful! Splendid! Full of creativity, and her artwork's just bursting with artistic merit! Law! Know what she said?"

"Who?" Sharalee asked with her mouth full of cookies and cornmeal. "Who are you even talking about?"

"Adrienne Dabney. Adrienne Dabney! Look." I pointed down at my feet.

"What you got there?" She drew in her breath and choked on the chips or something. "Girl, is that my friendship ring you got stuffed onto your fat old toe?" she asked, coughing and leaning over. "It is! I don't want my ring getting all smelly. Take it off."

"Sharalee, it's artistic. Anyone can wear a ring on her finger but only a creative spirit such as myself would wear it on her toe."

"Creative spirit? Since when?"

"You know I'm artistic. I've gotten an A in art every year of my life."

"Everyone gets A's in art, Charity."

"Yes, well, Adrienne said that I have the artist's eye, the way I stand back and observe the world. She said she noticed it right away the day she came over and she saw me go sit in the ladderback chair over in the corner. You know the one."

"Sure I do. The wobbly, breaking-apart ladderback. The one your daddy says you're supposed to take when there's company so they don't get it and discover it's just for show."

"So what? I would have taken it anyway, even if Daddy hadn't said. Adrienne says I'm an observer of life and someday I'm going to choose my art form and interpret my observations for all the world to see because I'll have this burning desire, this inner urging need to express myself, and most likely I'll have to go to Paris and New York City to do it. She says I got way too much spirit for a small town like Casper and someday, someday soon I'll have to spread my wings and fly." I spun around with my arms spread out and banged into one of the coffins.

Sharalee laughed. "No, you won't. Your daddy won't let you get any farther than Birmingham. You'll go to that Bible college they got there and become a preacher lady, just like you said. Remember?"

"Sharalee, hush."

"Remember you said you had the Holy Spirit come over you in that church in Atlanta where your father preached once? The big one with all the stained-glass windows? Remember you said how the sun shot through one of those windows and burned down on your head as if God Almighty Himself were breathing down on you?"

"Seems to me you forgot about the flat tire we had on the way back home from there and how all that Holy Spirit just whooshed right out of me like the air in that tire."

"I remember, all right, but you were so full of being holy you went and told your daddy right off and now he's spread it all over how you're going to follow in his footsteps, and just see if you don't."

"You'll be the one who sees, Sharalee. Did you know Adrienne ran off to New York City when she was just sixteen? That's just two years older than us. She moved out from New Jersey and went to live with her aunt."

"Alabama isn't New Jersey."

"So?"

"So you think you can just move on to New York just easy as pie? Who would you live with? All your kin's right here."

"Adrienne. She said I could. She said when Casper just got too small I could stay with her in New York and really discover myself and my art. She calls me 'soul of my soul.' Did you ever? We're artistic soulmates. And soon as she's done with her sensory deprivation project she's going to give me an art lesson. She said for me to be drawing and practicing all this month so I'll be ready. Isn't it just so splendid? Really, Sharalee, isn't it marvelous?''

Sharalee stuffed another cookie into her mouth and rubbed her greasy hands on the sides of her shorts. "If you're such soulmates all of a sudden what are you doing out here with me? Anyway, I'm the artistic one. I make all my own clothes and you don't even know which end of the needle is—''

"Law, Charity, you better git on home, Daddy's pitching a fit!''

I turned around and saw my sister, Grace, and her best friend, Boo, standing in the hole in the wall, panting.

"What's going on?'' I asked, already hurrying around the coffins to the hole.

"All's I know is Daddy saw Mad Joe tending that Miss Adrienne's yard, 'cause Miss Adrienne hired him to do it, and Daddy went and said something to him and then Mad Joe said something that got Daddy plenty mad and he came home and said for me and Boo to find you and he said, 'This instant!' ''

Boo nodded his head in emphasis.

I didn't even say good-bye to Sharalee. I ran along to the house with Grace and Boo, and there was Daddy waiting for me out on the porch, pacing and jingling the change in his pockets.

He stopped when he saw us coming. "Boo, you run on home now," he said. "And, Grace, you git on in the house and have yourself a bath. You look as if you spent all day in the mud."

The two of them scattered, leaving me to face my daddy. He stood looking down on me from the top of the steps and his face wore such a dark fury I scrunched my toes down into the dirt to keep his look from knocking me over.

I cleared my throat and spoke up. "Grace said you were wanting to see me, so I hurried on home."

"You went to see Miss Dabney?"

"Yes, sir. You never said not to, did you?" I tried to remember. I tried to think back to what he said after Adrienne left that afternoon. I remembered him watching her step off the porch and walk out the drive. I saw him shake his head when she met up with Mad Joe and the two of them started talking in the middle of the road.

"Isn't it fitting," he had said. "The two of them meeting up." He shook his head again and said, "That woman's of the devil."

Then later at dinner he said something

about not consorting with the devil and he pounded the table, but I was thinking he was meaning in a general sense. Lots of times he worked on his sermons in his head at the dinner table and he'd just blurt out a sentence he was wanting to use and wouldn't even realize he'd spoken out loud.

"And what's this I hear about a picnic?" Daddy interrupted my thinking.

"Picnic?"

"Mad Joe's set one of his signs out at the end of Miss Dabney's drive all about a—a coming-out picnic. He said you gave Miss Dabney the idea."

My toes were now scrunching so hard the pain of it was shooting clear up the front of my legs.

"She was wanting a way to please you, Daddy. She said the two of you got off on the wrong foot and she feels that when she offended you she offended the whole town."

Daddy spread his legs apart and folded his arms across his chest. "And she's right."

"She said folks were dropping by to take back their pies and such, and they were saying how they were sorry to have bothered her and to forgive them for displaying such unwanted hospitality, and if she didn't want to be taken into the fold, far be it from them to be shoving her into it.

"She was just wanting a way to make it up to them, and so—well, I thought, well, the church picnic is so much fun and everybody comes and it's the biggest event of the year, so I thought—"

"You just thought another one in the middle of the hottest summer on record would be a good idea?"

"I didn't think of it that way. I was just—"

"You weren't thinking at all! My picnic is in the fall because so many of the older folks can't handle the heat. Think of Miss Tuney Mae."

I pinched at my leg and thought about Miss Tuney Mae, ninety if she's a day, and nothing but a mouth and bones.

"My picnic has had years of fine-tuning: where to park the cars, who brings what, time of year, time of day. That's why it works, that's why it's the event of the year. What does Miss Dabney think, she's going to step out her door come the end of July and there we'll all be with food in our hands?"

"I said I'd take care of the details." I said this so low I knew Daddy didn't hear me.

"What?"

I looked up at him. "Daddy, you're right. I wasn't thinking. I don't know what I'm going to do."

"You're going to pull the sign up and be done with it, is what. Either that or you can go fetch yourself a switch sized to fit the deed and have yourself a whipping."

"But I've already made arrangements." My voice was whining. "I talked to the Cobb sisters and they're setting up the grills, and Old Higgs is fishing up the catfish, and freezing it, and I've got—"

"The Cobb sisters!" Daddy started pacing and jingling his change again. Then he turned on me, throwing up his arms and knocking his glasses off center. "They'll blow the place up! Neither one of them's got a lick of sense."

"Daddy, please. Don't let this picnic fall apart. It can't. It just can't. I promised. And, really, Adrienne isn't of the devil, you'll see. She's in there fasting and everything, just like Jesus. In the Bible it says—"

"Just like Jesus! Child, don't you open your mouth again. Don't you say another blasphemous word, or I'll fetch the switch myself. Now, are you going to march yourself over there this instant and pull up that sign?"

"Yes, sir."

Daddy pointed at the road. "Then git!"

And I got, but once I got past the house I slowed down to a dragging crawl and cried the rest of the way there, just knowing the hurt that would be pounding in Adrienne's heart when she came out and saw there wasn't a forgiving soul in all of Casper.

3

I did as Daddy told me and removed the picnic sign from Adrienne's yard, and right away folks started rolling into our driveway wanting to see Daddy. They were all saying the same thing: Someone had taken away Daddy's picnic sign!

Miss Tuney Mae said, "And after you was setting this town a good example and turning the other cheek and all."

Mattie-Lynn Pettit nodded. "Forgiving Miss Adrienne and her New York rudeness is just plain Christian, and I'd like to know who in this town took down your sign."

Then Hank Dooley called out from his truck, "I'm just wanting to see what a woman deprived of her senses looks like."

And Old Higgs, standing in our driveway with his fishing pole in one hand and a cooler in the other, said, "I already caught me a mess of catfish. What am I going to do with it all, hold a raffle?"

Before the evening was over Daddy was saying how the picnic would certainly go on as planned and he would have Mad Joe make up a new sign. And by the time of Adrienne's coming-out and the picnic, Daddy was running the whole show like it was his idea all along, and never a word was said between us that it wasn't. But, law, it was a long thirty days.

Planning the picnic and teaching Vacation Bible School and drawing pictures for Adrienne to see helped fill up the days, but that still left the mornings and the evenings; it still left too much time for thinking about Mama.

Every morning I'd sit up in bed and sniff the air, hoping that Mama had arrived home in the early dawn and was downstairs frying up bacon and eggs for the family the way she used to. At night I'd lie awake wondering where she was, what she was doing, if she was missing me. I'd try to remember her voice, frightened that I could forget how it sounded in such a short time. She called a couple of times and both times it was so noisy in the background with Cousin Maggie and Aunt Nooney and them laughing and carrying on that Mama didn't hear half of what I said, and most of what she said back was, "What? What did you say?" I asked her when she was coming home. I asked her both times, and both times she said how much she missed me and then asked to speak to Grace.

Grace once asked Daddy when Mama was coming home, and he was so mad at her for bothering him with such a question he sent her off to her room to memorize seven Bible verses. From then on, Grace always looked at Daddy like she suspected him of hiding Mama away in the broom closet or something.

Vacation Bible School was only two weeks long, meaning I still had two more weeks to wait for that picnic, and if they didn't drag on like a sweatin' dog on a dusty trail! I couldn't set still long enough to do any decent drawing anymore, and I couldn't help myself, every day I had to walk over to the Dabney place just to see it. Scary thing was, the house still looked the same as it always had, standing out in the field, boarded up and leaning and all. If it weren't for Mad Joe keeping up the yard, and the new sign for the picnic, I would swear I had imagined the whole splendid, marvelous thing.

Finally the day arrived and the whole town was just buzzing and bustling with activity. I was cooking up some of Mama's chicken delish and looking out the kitchen window, and I could see Daddy rushing between the house and the church, sending folks off with chairs and tables and extra supplies and giving orders to everybody. I could see the stream of cars going down our street to the Dooleys' store for some sugar or eggs or flour so folks could make up their picnic specialties, and I could see Grace and Boo taking the shortcut to Adrienne's with a bag of charcoal between them, dropping it every few feet.

By eleven o'clock we were ready to go, and me and Daddy grabbed up Mama's chicken delish and the jug of iced tea and stuff and hopped in the car. Daddy was wanting to get over to Adrienne's before the Cobb sisters, Miss Becky and Miss Anna, had a chance to start up the grill, so we were speeding along fast as we could.

By the time we pulled onto Adrienne's

freshly mowed field, the fire was already going. Problem was, it wasn't in the grill.

'Course we didn't know what was going on at first. All we could see was Miss Becky chasing Miss Anna round and round. She had her accordion in her hands and was squeezing it in and out and holding it up in this peculiar way, like she was about to clobber Miss Anna over the head with it.

Grace and Boo were there, too, jumping up and down and shouting something. We couldn't tell what till Daddy pulled up onto the edge of the lawn and we both jumped out of the car. Then we could hear, clear as clear, Grace and Boo yelling, "Stop, drop, and roll! Stop, drop, and roll!"

Mad Joe was coming round the corner of the house with a hose in his hand, and the two Cobb sisters just kept screaming and running round in circles. That's when I noticed that Miss Anna's braid was on fire and I realized Miss Becky was trying to put it out with the air from her accordion.

Daddy must have realized what was going on about the same time as I did, 'cause he right away dove into the backseat of the car and pulled out the fat jug of iced tea. Then he charged after the sisters, unscrewing the lid and tossing it behind him as he went. When he caught up to them he held tight to the handle and the bottom of the jug and flung the iced tea at Miss Anna. By then Mad Joe had come along with the hose and he was spraying her and Daddy both, and Miss Anna just stood under the shower of iced tea and water, flapping her arms and kicking out her legs. She didn't stop screaming until Daddy yelled at Mad Joe and Mad Joe dropped the hose. Then, after a polite "Thank you, Able, thank you, Joe," she turned to Miss Becky and shouted, "It's out now, Sister, you can put down the accordion. Becky! I said it's out. Stop puffing that thing at me, it's out."

Daddy set down the jug, kicked his wet leg out to the side like a dog, and pointed his finger at the two women. "When you came by to pick up the grills this morning, what did I say to you?"

"I know—we heard you, Able, but you know Sister, here," Miss Anna said. "I turned my back for just a minute and she managed to set it on fire."

"You said to light the grill," Miss Becky replied, her accordion dangling from her hand like all the spirit had gone out of the thing.

"I said, '*Don't* light the grill.' *Don't* light the grill. *Don't!*"

"Oh," said Miss Becky.

After Daddy helped Miss Anna to her car so she could go home and change, we started up the grills and set up the food tables the Dooleys had dropped off.

Then folks started to arrive, and I could tell by the way they were calling out their windows, and kids and dogs were piling out of cars and hopping off the backs of pickups before they had even stopped moving, that every one of them was just as charged with excitement as I was. It was like we were welcoming home a famous explorer; and maybe that's what Adrienne was, 'cause nobody we knew had ever sat in the dark doing nothing for a whole month before.

Daddy was telling everybody where to park and where to put their food and who should be doing what; and Mad Joe was giving his own directions 'cause he didn't want anyone parking too near the house, where he had planted an herb garden as a surprise for Miss Adrienne. And looking at him all clean-shaven and proud and not drunk at all, I wondered at folks calling him Mad.

I stood over the grill and watched to see that the fire didn't get out of control again, and every single body had to stop by to ask me about Mama. Had I heard from her lately?

When was she coming home? Didn't we all just miss her so? After hearing the same old questions a million times I got to understanding why Daddy blew up at Grace. I wanted to send every one of those nosy-bodies off to memorize the whole Bible—frontwards and backwards.

I saw Old Higgs Holkum arrive with Sharalee and her family in their truck. Daddy allowed them to back into the driveway, and I knew that meant that Mr. Marshall had loaded up the coffin.

Now, no amount of arguing with Sharalee was going to convince me that a coffin turned into an ice chest wasn't about the tackiest thing going. Mrs. Marshall said it was promoting the business to keep a coffin in the truck bed, and why not put it to good use while they were about it. 'Course she was just pleased 'cause she could feed her husband up right proper with his own ice chest in the back. He wouldn't have to be stopping at any of those cheap restaurants with the floozy waitresses when he went on his trips to Birmingham and Mobile. He could just set in his truck and have a feed right from the coffin.

I watched as Daddy, Old Higgs, and Mr.

Marshall hauled the monster out of the truck and set it on one of the food tables.

"What's in it this time?" I asked Sharalee when she caught up to me.

"Catfish and cola, and don't start in on me about it, okay?"

"Don't you get tired of being reminded of death everywhere you go? I mean, it looks like we're at a wake here."

"Don't you get tired of being reminded of God everywhere you go?"

"No," I said.

"Well, then?"

Somehow I missed the connection, but I didn't have much time to think about it 'cause Miss Tuney Mae had arrived in her old Fleetwood and was yelling her usual "Hey, y'all, come get me out of this contraption."

Daddy pointed at me and Sharalee, and as we headed for the car Sharalee said, "See what I mean? You always have to be the good girl and go fetch Looney Tuney, 'cause God is watching you."

"Sharalee, just hush," I said. "And anyways, Daddy's not God."

"Says who?"

"Well, girls, how nice of you to help me," Miss Tuney Mae said, holding out her arms and waiting for us to pull her out. And we did, we yanked and pulled and hoisted her, and we finally got her out of her seat. Even if she is all bones, she's deadweight.

She stood up and looked around, fanning herself with her straw hat. "Ain't it a scorcher already? I can hardly breathe through all this heat. It's like I got a plug-a cotton jammed up my nose."

I knew I was going to feel guilty for the heat all day, what with the summer picnic really being my idea, and if Miss Tuney Mae dropped dead from it, it would be all my fault.

"How 'bout I fetch you a cola, Miss Tuney Mae," I offered as we guided her toward the tables so she could set down her bag filled with the world's best tea cakes you'd ever hope to eat. They looked like fat cookies and tasted like heaven, not too sweet, so you could just keep eating them one after another and never get sick, and never get sick of them.

"Cola? Where's the cola? I don't see any cola."

"Over yonder." Sharalee pointed at the coffin.

I squeezed Miss Tuney Mae's arm and

held her up extra good just in case she saw the coffin and dropped dead from the heat and the sight of death staring back at her.

She nodded her head. "A Co-Cola would be nice, thank you, Sharalee."

Sharalee gave me a look of *ha, ha,* and then headed for the coffin.

Miss Tuney Mae turned to me. "Charity, you can fetch me my chair. Here's the key. It's in the trunk. You just set it up under that tree yonder with the Dunn twins, and I'll be there directly I've put these cakes down and had a little chat with Sharalee's mama."

I was happy to do anything I could to make sure Miss Tuney Mae was comfy and cool, so I got the chair out of the trunk and headed out toward Mad Joe's daughters. I was uneasy about going out to them 'cause they had to be two of the strangest people I had ever met. They were in my class at school until Mad Joe took them out and let them be home-schooled. Both of them had sickle-cell anemia and were home sick more than they were ever at school anyway. Still they were the smartest two people I knew. The kids at school called them the Encyclopedia Sisters, and their ways did kind of keep people at a distance, but they never seemed to mind.

Long as they had each other, no one else much mattered.

"Hey, Vonnie. Hey, Velita," I said, setting down Miss Tuney Mae's chair and flopping into it. Law, it was a hot day.

"Hello, Charity. How are you this fine day?" Vonnie asked. She was the twin who talked. It was the only way I could tell them apart. The other one mumbled.

I nodded and pointed out to where their father was showing folks his herb garden. "Your daddy sure seems to be doing splendid today."

Vonnie's face lit up. "Yes, it's a mighty fine day for Papa."

"Only drunk six times this month," Velita mumbled.

"He's done a real good job on the fields here and, well, I haven't heard him out shooting at anything in a long time," I said.

"No, he's had to take care of Sister here, she's had one of our spells, you know."

I looked Velita up and down. Of the two she did look the yellowest; even under their dark skin I could see it. Usually they had skin like their mama's, as black as a blue plum; but now the yellow was taking over, and they had lots of sores on their legs. To look at those sores made my stomach kind of queasy.

I looked out at the picnic instead and saw my daddy shouting at some young'uns getting too close to the grills.

"So, did your daddy put you in the hospital again?" I asked. I was asking Velita, but I knew it would be Vonnie who answered.

"Oh, no, he's through with doctors. They can't cure us, you know."

"They can just kill us," Velita mumbled.

"But can't they help the pain and alleviate aggravations and such?"

Vonnie shook her head. "We don't need them for that, we've learned to do that with our minds."

"Uh-huh." See, they always started talking over my head eventually. A Frisbee landed at my feet and I bent over, picked it up, and tossed it back out toward the crowd.

"We overcome pain with prayer, Charity. You understand?" Vonnie shaded her eyes with her hand and looked at me. "Papa can't stand to see our pain. He's afraid of it, I think. He looks at it as if it's a separate living thing, a monster he has to slay. Understand?"

I nodded. "I reckon I do," I said. I wondered what Sharalee was saying to the right handsome Billy Gumm. She knew I liked him, and there the two of them were rolling cold soda cans across their foreheads and laughing with each other, and they weren't even noticing that the table with the coffin setting on it was starting to sink.

"We try not to let him know we're suffering."

I brought my mind back to what Vonnie was saying.

"People think he goes off on his drinking binges because of Mama's death, but really it's because he's afraid."

I glanced sideways at the twins. Anytime someone mentioned Datina's death I wondered if they got the same giggly feeling inside that I did. It wasn't funny, really it wasn't, 'cause after she died Mad Joe did take a turn for the worse and so did the twins; but see, the way Miss Tuney Mae tells it, how Datina died of claustrophobia in a Porta Potti at the Peanut Festival, well, she makes it sound awful funny when it wasn't at all, I'm sure.

"I'm sorry, Vonnie, Velita. I am." And I was.

"He's afraid of us dying," Velita said.

I stared bug-eyed at Velita. I'd never heard her speak so loud, but then again Miss Becky was getting close with her accordion and Velita was having to talk over "Love Makes the World Go Round," the only song Miss Becky knew.

"He doesn't understand we're ready. He's looking for some miracle to save us, but we want to be with Mama. Don't we, Sister?" Velita took her sister's hand in hers.

Vonnie nodded. " 'Take my body who will, it is not me.' "

"Huh?"

"From *Moby Dick,* did you ever read it?"

"No, not lately," I said, thinking it was time I got back to the picnic.

Vonnie kissed her sister's knuckles and said, " 'Methinks my body is but the lees of my better being. In fact take my body who will, take it I say, it is not me.' "

I nodded and tried to change the subject so I could leave without them thinking I was wanting to get away from their death talk, which I was. "Well, your daddy's done a splendid job here."

"Yes." Vonnie's voice was brighter. "You know he's put in a vegetable garden out back. Papa says Miss Adrienne's going to need those vegetables after her fasting all month on water and fruit juice."

"Probably had diarrhea all month," Velita mumbled.

"I wonder if she even remembers there's going to be a picnic," I said.

"Oh yes," Vonnie said. "You know, every day she slipped a piece of paper under the door just to let Papa know she was all right. If there was no paper, then Papa was to use the key she gave him and go in and get her. He's got thirty pieces of paper in his pocket."

"Really?" I was surprised Adrienne would trust Mad Joe to even be there every day, and I was a little hurt that she didn't make the arrangement with me instead. After all, I was the one who sat out on her back porch one whole afternoon, drinking iced coffee and eating grapes and learning about being an artist. I was the artistic one. I was the soul of her soul.

"Yes, really," Vonnie said. "Today, Papa slipped a paper under her door telling her what day it was and that the picnic was to take place as planned and that he would come get her out at noon exactly. And look at Papa. He keeps checking his watch and strutting around. This is a big day for him. He hasn't been this lively since before Mama died."

Vonnie looked down at her watch. Velita

looked down at hers. "Just fifteen minutes and Papa will go let her out."

I stood up. I had always imagined I would be the one to let Adrienne out. I could see it, her barely able to walk from a month of deprivation, and having to lean on me as I escorted her outside, where folks would be running up and gathering round. It was going to be a great moment, and now that moment was going to be Adrienne's and Mad Joe's.

"I reckon I'll start over there so I won't miss all the excitement," I said to the twins. "Y'all coming?"

"No, thank you, Charity, we'll wait here. Daddy will fetch us directly."

I left the twins and headed back to the crowd. I saw Mad Joe look at his watch and then start trotting out toward me. He nodded when he passed but went on to fetch his daughters.

Daddy had the spatula in his hand and was banging it on the side of the grill. He had an announcement to make, he said. I hurried to catch up with the others.

Daddy quoted Scripture, saying what Miss Tuney Mae had said about turning the other cheek and how Jesus said we must not forgive a person once or even seven times, we must forgive seventy times seven; and everyone clapped and Miss Becky started up "Love Makes the World Go Round" again and Daddy shouted above it all, "It is now time for me to let Miss Adrienne out."

I tried to call to him. I tried to push through the folks and past the tables to tell him about Mad Joe, but it was too late. Daddy was pounding on the door. And, law, how the folks were cheering and gathering round Daddy. I looked back and I saw Mad Joe half running and half slowing down to stay in step with his daughters. He was shouting something, but no one could hear. They were too busy shouting, "Surprise!" Adrienne had come out of her house!

4

Adrienne came out before I even had a chance to turn back around. And when I did, there she was, squinting and laughing and hugging folks like she had known them for years. And they were hugging her back and laughing and saying "Welcome" and "Surprise" over and over again, and Miss Becky was playing "Love Makes the World Go Round." Then they grabbed Adrienne away from Daddy and led her out toward the picnic tables. Adrienne was stepping carefully 'cause she was barefoot and the grass was dry and sharp. She was looking around like she had lost something.

Then she saw Mad Joe and waved and he waved back, smiling and motioning for her to go on with the group that was pulling her to the tables. And I was tagging along behind everybody, feeling just like Macy, the Dooleys' three-legged dog.

They let Adrienne go first through the line and everyone else lined up behind her with their paper plates. And they were shouting and showing off to Adrienne, saying how she had to try their fresh tomato-bean salad, or their corn pudding, or whatever. And Adrienne was loading up her plate and saying how she had had enough fruit juice to last her a lifetime and how food never looked so good. This pleased everybody so much they insisted she didn't look pale or thin or anything, when really she did.

I piled up my plate with a stack of Mrs. Marshall's cornbread, the corn pudding, one of Old Higgs's catfish, some of Miss Tuney Mae's tea cakes, and a cup of Mattie-Lynn Pettit's iced tea, 'cause hers was always made with extra sugar and not too much lemon.

Everyone had already filled in the seats next to Adrienne, so I had to go sit at one of the children's tables with Sharalee, all the Dooleys' young'uns, and Vonnie and Velita.

"Hey, Vonnie, Velita, sorry about your daddy and all," I said, ashamed to look at them.

"It's all right, Charity, he's sitting with her now," Vonnie said, smiling.

I twisted around to see and got an earful of laughter and applause and, law, I was wishing I was sitting over there.

I turned back around. "So anyway, how do you like taking your schooling at home?" I asked them, trying to keep my mind busy.

"We like it fine when we're feeling well, but it's lonely," said Vonnie. "Why don't you and Sharalee come visit us?"

I looked over at Sharalee, who was giving me a *now-you've-done-it* look, and then back at Vonnie.

"Sorry, Vonnie. I guess it's because—I don't know why—your daddy and all, I guess."

"Grace and Boo come see us," Velita whispered to her chicken delish.

Yeah, well, they would, I thought to myself, but since Velita just whispered about Grace and Boo, I decided to pretend I didn't hear.

Sharalee shoved at Cal Dooley, who was trying to poke his finger in her plate of Jell-O salad, and then said to the twins, "May I ask what subjects you have been studying since leaving our fine class last November?"

I swanee, Sharalee can be a real noodle sometimes. She was the one who started calling them the Encyclopedia Sisters and of course after she did, everyone did.

"We're doing a lot of reading mostly, Sharalee," Vonnie said. "Have you read *Wuthering Heights?*"

Sharalee and I both shook our heads.

"You'd love it, I'm sure of that." Vonnie smiled but looked sideways at Velita, who was mumbling something about studying calculus and physiology and Mary Baker Eddy.

"If you like poetry," Vonnie continued, "you might try Emily Dickinson. She's quite easy to understand. You know, she lived all her adult life in her house and never got out to see anyone."

Sharalee and I nodded and probably looked to her like two dumb sacks of feed sitting across from her.

I caught Velita saying something to her iced tea about Dickinson living in a mansion and them in a shack and how it wasn't the same as them at all.

Actually they lived in a shotgun house:

two rooms, one behind the other, so you could stand in the front doorway and fire a bullet straight through the house and out the back door without it running into anything on its way out. Mad Joe had posted a sign out front that said their house was just like the house Elvis Presley was born in and people were free to take a tour if they wanted. 'Course it just being two rooms and kind of rundown to boot, it wasn't much to see, but I always had a nice feeling whenever I passed that sign, like if Elvis could make it all the way from his shotgun house to Graceland, then maybe I could make it out of Casper, someday.

I heard someone calling my name and looked up to see Adrienne standing at her table, waving to me and calling me over. When I got there, all red in the face, I'm sure, Adrienne put her arm around me and announced how me and Mad Joe were the ones who helped her prepare for her experiment and how she owed the success of it to us.

"I was telling everyone how my month in isolation went and I thought you'd want to hear, too," she said to me.

"Sure I do." I grinned at the group gathered around and then she began her story, trying to talk to everyone over my head until I caught Daddy's eyeball motions and sat down in Adrienne's chair.

"I tell you, those first several days I just about went crazy," she began. "I mean, what can a person do who can't hardly see or hear or feel or smell? I'll tell you what I did. I soaked myself in a lot of cold, cold baths—the heat was something."

Folks laughed at that and Adrienne rested her hands on my shoulders and went on.

"I also talked a lot. I was talking constantly. 'Well, now, Adrienne,' I'd say, 'how about a little meditation? How about going upstairs now? How about washing your hair?' It wasn't until about what I'd guess was the second week that I stopped talking to myself and just listened to the silence. It's amazing what a person can hear in the silence."

People were nodding their heads like they sat listening to the silence every minute of their lives.

"After a while it was all I really had, that silence. I wasn't talking or seeing, and wasn't even eating. I stopped keeping track of whether it was day or night, and believe it or not, I didn't seem to be sleeping or dreaming much, either. I spent more and more time meditating. I had this special spot in my house where I went each time, drawn there by habit, I suppose, but it was the only place where I could really calm myself. During those times when I'd start going crazy just being by myself, I'd find myself wandering over to that spot, sitting down, resting my hands in my lap, and then, *sssssss*—all the craziness would run right out of me."

I noticed that all the kids had gathered on the grass behind the adults and were listening to Adrienne like she was telling them a bedtime story. The adults from the other table had turned their chairs around to listen better as well, and I felt all squiggly and excited inside as if it were me who had done all this, as if I were the one telling the story.

Adrienne took her hands off my shoulders and I turned around. Her eyes were sparkling and her face was red and sweaty and happy, and I knew, I just knew, she was about to tell us something special, something no one else had ever said before.

She took this deep smiley breath and sucked all this air between her teeth before she continued. Then she closed her eyes and said, "One time I had been sitting in my spot who knows how long, and I noticed this glow in front of me." She opened her eyes and tilted her head. "I stared at it for a long time and I could see it was my chair, my little wooden chair with the rush seat, and it was all lit up. I looked at the space around the chair and there was nothing there, just gray space, everywhere this gray space. My eyes were drawn back to the chair and it was getting brighter, and the brighter it got, the better I felt, you know? Warm and safe and loved and calm and happy all at the same time. Then the light changed. It started circling around the chair, moving and growing until the light took form. I can't believe what I saw." Adrienne opened her eyes wider, looked around at all of us with her mouth open and her shoulders shrugged up around her ears.

"He was in my chair," she said. "He was sitting in my chair! Jesus Christ was sitting in my chair!"

5

Daddy was the first to react to Adrienne's revelation. He jumped up. His chair fell backwards to the ground and he shouted at the quiet faces staring up at him, "Stay calm, everybody, just stay calm!"

Mattie-Lynn Pettit was the only one who moved. She leaned over and picked up Daddy's chair. "It's okay, Able," she said.

Daddy looked to his left and right real fast and then lowered himself down into his chair. He nodded to Adrienne. "Go on," he said.

Adrienne opened her mouth to speak but Miss Becky spoke up first.

"What did He look like?" she asked. "Did He look like that handsome Jesus in the stained window at the church?"

"Now, Becky, you know that's just some artist's painting. What would a man born in Bethlehem be doing with blue eyes and red hair?" Miss Anna gave her sister a squeeze that was loving but also meant *Shut up*.

"But that's just the sun making it so red, isn't it, Able? I'm sure that's just what He looked like. Didn't He, Adrienne?"

"Well, actually—" Adrienne started to speak again but this time everyone started talking at once, giving their neighbors an earful of what they thought Jesus looked like.

Things were starting to get out of hand, with folks standing up and shouting and grabbing up plates of dessert and stuffing food down their throats and spitting it back out as they shouted some more.

Daddy looked as if he were about to stand up on his chair and shout for everyone to calm down again. I was worried that as soon as he got up there everyone would have somehow shut up and taken their seats, and he'd be standing up there like he thought he looked just like the real Jesus and that everyone should see.

He climbed up there with Mattie-Lynn holding on to the chair, and finally he got everyone settled down except Miss Becky, who was asking in a loud whisper if Miss Anna thought Jesus looked like the Jesus in the stained window.

"Miss Becky," Daddy said, still standing on the chair, "let's hear what Miss Adrienne has to say about *her* Jesus now."

We all turned back to Adrienne.

"Well, actually I couldn't tell you what He looked like. It's a funny thing . . ." Adrienne paused and squinted up into the sun. Then she looked back down at all of us. "He was there. I knew it was Jesus, I could feel Him, I could see Him—in a sense—but—but I haven't the words, there aren't the words to explain. I'm sorry, I wish I could tell you He wore white robes and had long red hair and blue eyes"— she glanced over at Miss Becky—"but all I can say is that He—He just *was*."

Adrienne's hands were shaking and her eyes were looking all over the place. I got the feeling that she wished she hadn't ever mentioned the Jesus thing at all.

"I—Maybe I shouldn't have told you all this," she said. Which just goes to show that one of us was reading the other's thoughts.

"It's just that I think Jesus was here for a reason. I—I mean, I'm not a Jesus person, and yet I saw things. Jesus showed me. I know these things and—and I'm not sure what I'm supposed to do about them—really." She looked around at all of us like she was waiting for us to tell her what to do.

I turned around to find Daddy, figuring he would have something to say. He was still standing up on the chair, with an expression on his face that looked like someone had just stomped on his bunion or something. I turned back around, hoping no one else would look for him.

Then Adrienne spoke again. "The first time it happened—the first time Jesus came to the chair—I felt so—so new, so good, exhilarated. Then when it was all over and I was left to myself again and time went by, I began to wonder, did it really happen?" She gave us a questioning look like one of us was going to tell her.

"Then I wondered, why me? Why did Jesus come to me? What was He trying to say to me? He came two more times, each time more fantastic than the next, and now, today, I wonder, how am I supposed to have changed? I'm so full of all these new feelings.

I know things, I know these things, but it's still the same me. I'm no different." She gave a quick laugh and shrugged her shoulders.

Jim Ennis stood up. "I want to see this chair of yours," he said.

Then everyone was getting up again and shouting about the Jesus chair and marching toward the house like they were going to roust out some lawbreaker and hang him.

I saw this dark flash of somebody speed past me, past all of us, and by the time we got to the front door, there was Mad Joe leaning against the door, facing us and panting, his nostrils going in and out real fast, and his eyes all wild looking. It shut us all up right fast.

When he saw that we were all silent he spoke to us in this scratchy voice. "Y'all can't just go trampling in this house without an invite." He glared at Jim Ennis and the Dooley brothers, who looked like they were ready to bust right through poor Mad Joe and start gnawing on the Jesus chair with their bloodthirsty teeth. "Y'all back up and see reason," he said to them.

"A fine thing, you telling us to see reason, madman," Hank Dooley yelled.

Mad Joe stayed calm. "What if Jesus was looking down on us right now, what if? What would He say, I wonder? Would He say, 'Now, there's a group of decent folks lovin' their neighbor'? No sir, He'd say, 'Folks never learn, they sure don't. They haven't learned a dad-burned thing.' That's what He'd say."

We kind of backed away a bit after Mad Joe said that, and Jim and the Dooleys tried to slip back into the crowd like they could hide from Jesus.

"Maybe," Mad Joe went on, "maybe if we was to ask nice, Miss Adrienne would let us each take a look at her chair. At a later time—'cause I'm sure we ain't gonna see Jesus setting there waiting for us now—no sir, no sir. Miss Adrienne was setting in silence when she heard that 'still, small voice,' and if y'all plan on seeing or hearing the good Lord, I s'pect y'all better muster up some silence, too, and go on in to see that chair with reverence."

"Look who's telling us what," I heard someone say.

"Yeah," a few others said, taking a couple of steps back toward Mad Joe.

Then Daddy stepped forward and stood in front of Mad Joe, facing us. "All right, everybody. Let's not get carried away with this thing."

"We're just wanting a look, Able," Mr. Marshall said.

Everyone was standing there nodding and

saying, "Yeah, we just want to see," and such like that, but Daddy held up his hands.

"There's nothing to see. There's nothing to see. Y'all hear a story like this and right away you're wanting to bust through the door without thinking things through. I can promise you, Jesus is not waiting for you in any chair."

Was Daddy thinking Adrienne was a liar? I turned to look for Adrienne. I saw her at the back of the group. She was turned the other way, with her head bent forward. Was she crying? I pushed through the crowd real hard and almost knocked Sharalee over doing it.

"Hey, Charity, what—"

"Y'all leave!" I shouted through Sharalee's remark. "Just leave. You're ruining it. Miss Adrienne shares something wonderful and splendid, and you just kill it. Leave!" I shouted at them. I was crying when I turned to my daddy. "Daddy, make them leave. Just make them leave." Then I burst through the crowd again and ran. I didn't hear what anyone was saying behind me, I just knew they were talking. I kept on running, past the picnic tables and all the cars, across the street, and into the cornfields.

6

The next day was Sunday, and on Sundays it was my job to see that Grace didn't wander off before church. This meant that I always had to get up before sunrise, 'cause Grace always did, and if I didn't, she'd be out the door and rolling around in the wire-grass swamp and I'd be the one Daddy would blame. Problem was, the picnic left me so frizzy-frazzied I could hardly cope with my usual Sunday morning routine with the curling iron, hair gel, makeup, dress, stockings, and high heels. And this Sunday was supposed to be special. This Sunday I had planned to unveil my new look. Now, with what happened yesterday and Daddy likely to be furious with me and the world, I wasn't so sure it was such a good idea.

I studied the skirt and shawl lying on my bed and thought about how just two nights ago I was so excited about the outfit I couldn't stand still. Sharalee, the best seamstress on this planet, had been trying to pin the hem up while I was grabbing the shawl she had already finished. I'd wrapped it around my shoulders like I was a model and struck a pose, sucking in my cheeks and pointing my right foot.

"Charity, if you don't quit I'm going to stick you," Sharalee said.

"Ow!"

"Well, see there? Now stay still. I swanee, the things I let you talk me into!"

"You said your mama wasn't using these bedspreads anymore. You did ask her if you could have them, didn't you?" I was starting to panic, thinking of Mrs. Marshall seeing me in her bedspreads at church and whirling them off me with one quick yank. I could just picture myself spinning out into the aisle and then coming to a standstill in front of the right handsome Billy Gumm in nothing but my underwear.

"What would my mama want with these old things? India-print stuff went out of style years ago." Sharalee stuck another pin in the skirt and popped a rolled-up wad of bread in her mouth.

I examined the fringe Sharalee had sewn along the edge of the shawl. "I think it's cool. It's the new me."

"It's the old Adrienne Dabney's what it is, Charity," she mumbled around the bread. "And you know it and so will your papa."

"Well, maybe so, but it's the new me."

"Your daddy would say, if you want to change, you have to start from the inside and then the outside just takes care of itself."

"First of all, Daddy puts it a lot better than that, and second of all, he's talking about the changes that happen when you let Jesus into your life, and third of all, since when do you listen to any of Daddy's sermons?"

"You're not the only one who's changing in this town, miss artsy-smartsy. There now, I'm done." She gulped down the last of her iced tea and I saw the glop of undissolved sugar slip along the glass and into her mouth.

"Law, Sharalee, that's disgusting!"

"Since when? Now, turn around and let me make sure the hem's even before I sew it in."

Right before I left her house, the precious outfit tucked under my arm in a grocery bag, Sharalee dared me to wear it to church on Sunday.

Now here it was Sunday and I was planning to do my first ever back-down on a Sharalee Marshall dare.

I picked up the shawl and wrapped it around me. I pushed aside the large wicker birdcage setting on my bureau and studied myself in the mirror. I noticed how the blue in the print made my eyes look more blue and less "seaworthy gray," as Mama called them.

"Adrienne wouldn't worry about what everyone would say," I told my reflection. I flipped my head forward, then back, to make my hair fluff out more, and then raised my eyebrows to make them look arched like Adrienne's. "What's that, Father dear? You say I look like a tramp?" I gave my reflection an Adrienne laugh. "Nonsense. I'm just young, Father dear. I'm free. I'm an artist." I nodded to myself. "Yes, I'm an artist. I'm an artist. I'm not a preacher lady. I'm a preacher's daughter and I'm an artist." I tossed one long end of the shawl over my shoulder, told myself I wasn't going to back down from this no matter what Daddy said, and turned back to the skirt.

I kept my nerve all the way through putting on the skirt and tank top, with no bra, and all the way through not curling my hair but just sort of teasing it to get it to look a bit wilder, and even all the way through not putting on the stockings, which really everyone should have thanked me for 'cause I hadn't washed them all year, but I lost it right quick when I started for the stairs and heard Daddy arguing with Mama on the phone. I sat up on the top stairs and listened.

"It's obvious you've never heard of resting on the Sabbath," Daddy was saying.

"What do you mean, you're not just a preacher's wife? Of course you are, and I'd like to know what gets into you at those conventions." Daddy listened a minute and then in a raised voice he said, "I know you're not still at the convention. How very well I know it!" He paused, listening again, and then said, "Now, what kind of wild talk is that?" And then, getting angrier and wilder himself, he said, "I think y'all had better come on home. Yes, now. This instant! No, I'm not ordering you, I'm just saying . . ." Daddy listened again for a long while, and I thought about their last fight.

It happened about a week before Mama left for the Birdcage Collectors' Convention.

That morning Mama had gone off to the Dooleys' store for some coffee and toilet tissue, and didn't come back till dinnertime. Turned out she had gone shopping with Aunt Nooney. She claimed she'd run into her at Dooleys' and they just took off on a whim. Daddy said she had been having too many whims lately and it was time she took hold of herself before it got out of hand. Daddy was right, too, 'cause she had been coming home with all kinds of useless stuff. One time she brought home eight bags filled with yellow plastic tulips. She said she was going to fill some of her larger birdcages with them but she never did. Another time she bought several boxes of preemie diapers and Daddy wanted to know if now she was planning to diaper the cages. Mama just fell over hysterical with laughter, which got us all upset, 'cause Mama never thought Daddy was funny before, and she was acting different, not her quiet self atall.

Then the time they had their last fight, there we were all in the kitchen finishing up dinner when Mama came in with three bags filled with what must have been a whole display of Christmas socks. Mama said she got them way marked down since it was almost summer, but Daddy didn't care. He called her behavior outlandish and wanted to know the meaning of it all. And Mama said, "There is no meaning. That's what I like about it. I just bought them." Mama tossed the bags onto the kitchen table, just missing Grace's glass of milk, flopped down in her chair, and said, "I'm tired of everything having meaning, Able." And she looked tired, too. She had been looking tired all the time lately, up until the day she started packing for the convention. Her eyes were droopy looking and her mouth couldn't hold a smile for more than a second, as if her smile were broken from having to use it so much being the preacher's wife. She was going round in a pair of shoes with the heels so worn down on the outside they made her feet slant sideways, and the hem of her favorite brown skirt had come down in the back and she wore it every day anyway.

Daddy told her that he didn't like the changes going on with her, and Mama said Daddy didn't like any kind of change and that was his whole problem. She said, "Everything changes, Able, but you keep trying to hold everything still, pin the whole world down, and you can't. If things don't change they just up and die, and I'm tired of dying. I'm just so tired of it all."

Well, Grace heard that about Mama dying

and took off from the table, and Daddy said, "Now see what you've done? You've upset the child."

But it wasn't Mama that Grace was upset with, it was Daddy. She said it was all Daddy's fault Mama was dying, and no amount of reminding her how much Daddy loved Mama and explaining about figures of speech and such could change Grace's mind.

I got so caught up with remembering Daddy and Mama fighting and listening in on their phone conversation that when Daddy said good-bye in this real quiet voice and put down the receiver, I headed on into the kitchen to ask Daddy about Mama coming back and forgot all about my new outfit.

Daddy's hand was still on the receiver, his head bent forward, when I came clomping in wearing the sandals Sharalee had loaned me. Each step made a loud *clomp-clomp* sound on the wood floor, and when I heard them I remembered what I had on and just froze in my tracks. Daddy lifted his head and stared at me like he was catching sight of Lady Godiva with a head shave.

I could feel my face burning but then I thought of how Adrienne stood up in front of all those folks the day before, like she just had a right to do so, and I looked straight at my daddy's face and said, "Morning, Daddy, hope you had a good night's sleep. Mmm, what's for breakfast? I smell something good."

I walked over to the table and with my back to him pulled my chair out. I was about to set down when I felt the chair jerked out from under me. I turned back around and I swanee, what I saw, it wasn't my daddy atall. It was just this monster in Daddy's beige suit and hairpiece. This purple-faced, blood-drooling ape-man was fighting with the chair like it was alive and trying to strangle him. He picked it up with both hands and snarled and yanked it around several times as if he were trying to wad it up into a wooden ball so he could throw it at someone. Then he threw it down and kicked it across the room, pounded on it, and did that fighting yanking thing again. He hit his head on the pink birdcage hanging from the ceiling and his glasses flew off and slid across the floor, but he just kept going at that chair. Then he turned toward me with such fury in his face and pain in his eyes I screamed and flew out of the kitchen and up those stairs. I tore at my outfit like it was on fire. I ignored all the ripping sounds and just kept tearing until it was all off. I heard someone on the stairs and I slammed my door and screamed some more. I screamed while I scraped the comb through my hair and screamed when I saw big clumps of my hair dropping to the dresser. I screamed into my bra and I screamed into last year's sundress with the daisies on it. I screamed into my stockings and screamed when I shredded the left side of the stockings with one of my fingernails and had to take them off. I pulled on the first pair of socks I could find, not caring even if they matched so long as my shoes didn't pinch. Then, feeling dressed to Daddy's satisfaction, I opened my door, ran past someone in the hall, screamed down the stairs and out the side door.

7

I didn't stop running until I reached the grave-
yard that lay between our house and the
church. My whole body was still shaking and
my throat hurt from all my screaming. I set
down on the grass and leaned against one of
the gravestones. I thought maybe I'd just stay
out there forever, maybe just melt into the
ground next to one of the dead people. I
couldn't stop crying.

"Is that just you, Charity?" I heard Boo
whisper from somewhere behind me.

I jumped up and spun around, looking
for him while I answered. "Well, who do

you think it is, some ghost? Where are you? Grace? Boo?"

Boo stepped out from behind a huge block of granite. Grace stepped out behind him.

"We thought maybe it was the reverend," Grace said.

"The reverend? Does Daddy know you're calling him that?" I wiped the tears off my face.

Grace didn't answer.

I turned on Boo, who stood there looking like a ghost himself in all his baldness. The boy didn't have a hair on his body. Miss Tuney Mae claimed it was because his mama had had some awful fright when he was still in her womb and it caused the both of them to lose their hair; only difference was she got to wear a wig.

"Law, Boo, don't be creeping up on me like that, you hear? Anyway, what are you two up to? I thought you were supposed to be out on the porch, shelling peas."

"We were just wondering what's wrong with the reverend," Boo said.

"Nothing. What do you mean, what's wrong?"

Boo's eyes sort of rolled around in his head a few times, and then he said, "Why was he so angry? You were screaming. Did he beat you?"

I looked at Grace. " 'Course not. I swanee, Grace, don't you set him straight on anything?"

Grace just shrugged. "We were scared," she said.

"What are you two inventing now? Calling Daddy the reverend and then thinking he's in there beating me up. Lordy-loo, Grace, you ought to know better."

"I've never seen him so angry," Grace muttered. "We saw through the window. We were scared."

"What was he so mad about?" Boo asked again.

"I don't know. I don't know—maybe 'cause Mama's gone, or maybe he didn't like what I had on, or maybe it was that Jesus chair thing, I don't know. Does there have to be a reason anymore? Seems to me that lately he's just angry to be angry. Law, what I wouldn't give to be with Mama right now— to be anywhere but here."

I turned away from them, walking out of the cemetery and the yard and down the road toward the cornfields. Grace and Boo followed behind me like spies. I walked faster, feeling the sweat on my forehead and under my arms building up to a couple of good trickles. The two of them trotted up alongside of me. I didn't say anything to them and they didn't seem to expect me to, so we marched on in silence, stomping around the cornfields and down the street. I heard a train hooting down the tracks that cut across the road about a half mile away, and its call made something inside me squeeze until I thought I wouldn't be able to take another breath.

Then Grace poked my shoulder and said, "Look, there's Mad Joe."

Sure enough, there he was, down on his knees in front of Adrienne's house, digging in the herb bed and singing some kind of lonesome song.

"Law, if he's got his shotgun we're running the other way," I said.

"He wouldn't shoot us, Charity," Boo said. "We ain't worms."

"Yes, but in his usual Sunday-morning condition we might just look like worms to him. Now I mean it, you two, you stay with me."

"He doesn't look in his usual Sunday condition, though," Grace said. "He's just digging."

"Hey, Mad Joe!" Grace and Boo both called out.

Mad Joe raised up from the garden and waved his trowel.

Grace and Boo took off and were down on their knees digging beside him before I could catch hold of either one of their shirts and stop them.

I hurried across the lawn to catch up.

"Hey, Mr. Joe Dunn, sir," I said, standing behind the three of them, my eyes searching the truck bed beside us for his shotgun.

Mad Joe twisted himself around and sat back on his heels. "Well, gracious me, Charity, look at you. You 'bout as tall as your daddy, I'm thinking." Mad Joe had this delighted look on his face like he was really glad to see me.

I smiled back. "Yes, sir, I am. I'm five foot seven."

"That's good. Yes, siree, that sure is."

Then both of us looked at each other like we were each waiting for the other to say something else.

Mad Joe took off his hat and set it on Boo's head.

Boo lifted his head. "I can't see."

Mad Joe laughed, this *he-he-he* kind of

laugh. "You keep it on anyway. You oughtn't to be going round without a hat on, Mr. Boo— and be careful with that rosemary, it ain't holding up so well." He turned back to me. "You here to see the Jesus chair?"

Funny thing, I didn't know why I was there. I hadn't meant to be going anywhere special and then there I was. But now that he asked me, I was wanting awful bad to see the chair, to talk to it.

"Yes, sir," I said.

Mad Joe rubbed his hands together and clumps of dirt dropped to the ground.

"It's a miracle, it sure is," he said.

"Yes, sir."

"I knew it, too. You know that? I knew Miss Adrienne was a messenger sent from Datina."

"Datina—your wife, you mean?" I asked.

"Yes, ma'am, my wife." Mad Joe nodded. "She always telling me to have the faith. Always saying, 'Don't give up on our babies.' Always saying to expect a miracle, and I been waiting. I been waiting on her to send down a miracle, 'cause I know no doctor'll cure my babies—and then, soon as I set eyes on this Miss Adrienne, I knew my Datina was working a miracle. My babies got a book full of paintings of angels, and don't every one of them look like this Miss Adrienne. So I been here every day waiting. Been waiting just to see what my Datina would do next, and Lord have mercy, she done sent me a Jesus chair. Now, you just see if my babies don't get a cure." He turned back around and started digging again, taking the trowel away from Boo and sending him off to fetch the watering can.

I heard a door slam and saw Adrienne coming off her back porch toward us. My heart did a flip-flop. She was shuffling toward us wearing this huge flowery kimono in turquoise and orange and red, and I just had chills watching her, 'cause there she was just letting about a half foot of it trail in the dirt without a care. Now, that's living. Daddy wouldn't let me so much as drag my feet, let alone some elegant piece of clothing. Someday, I thought to myself, someday I'm going to have enough money to buy myself something silky and expensive, and then I'm going to drag it everywhere like it's just an old dishrag.

Adrienne caught up to us and put her arm around me and nodded at Mad Joe.

Mad Joe jumped to his feet. "Morning," he said. "I hope we weren't disturbing your slumbering. I was just wanting to set some of these plants right after yesterday's trampling."

Adrienne laughed and shook out her hair. It had been tied in a knot, and just with the one shake of her head, out it came. I couldn't wait to try that in front of my mirror.

"Thank you, Joe," she said in her ice-melting voice. "I thought you might want to go in to see the chair. You said yesterday . . ."

Mad Joe smiled. "Yes, ma'am. I would, that's a fact. I just got to dip my hands in this here bucket and wash 'em off."

Mad Joe reached down and rubbed his hands together in the water. Then he wiped them on the towel he had wrapped around his neck, picked himself some of the rosemary, and gave a little bow. "Excuse me, won't you," he said. Then he hurried round to the back porch, and we waited but he didn't slam the screen door. He just let it gently creak shut.

Grace and Boo both stood up, dusting off their hands. Boo pushed Mad Joe's hat back off his face and studied Adrienne. Just when I was really starting to squirm 'cause he was staring so hard, he said, "The reverend's going to be talking about you this morning."

"About me? About my visions, you mean?"

Grace and Boo both nodded.

"About the Rapture," Boo said. "We heard him talking about it this morning, didn't we, Grace?"

Adrienne gave Boo a real hard look, studying him all over. Maybe she was just getting around to noticing he had no eyebrows or something, but I had a feeling it was more 'cause of the Rapture thing.

"Folks are saying this could be it," Grace said. " 'Course the reverend doesn't agree. He said it would take more than this kind of thing to fool this town."

"What?" Adrienne's face went all chalky. "What are you talking about. Rapture? What's rapture?"

"Rapture. You know, Jesus' second coming. Miss Becky Cobb was saying yesterday how this is it. The time is nigh." Boo blinked at Adrienne. "She came by our place last night all fidgety fingered. She said she was just making sure one of us hadn't gone up into the clouds yet 'cause she's wanting to make sure when people start going she knows it so she can be ready. She hates surprises, Miss Becky does. They make her real nervous. 'Course my daddy says with all the fires she's been setting lately, she's likely to really get a surprise when she's one of the ones left standing on the ground jest a-weeping and a-gnashing her teeth."

Adrienne tightened the silk sash around her waist and looked at the three of us with such choking bewilderment it's a wonder she could stay standing.

I tried to explain. "The Rapture is when Jesus returns after a lot of wars and evildoings and judges both the dead and live folks and chooses which ones He's wanting with Him and which ones will be left behind to suffer. He takes all the good, true believers up with Him."

"The Rapture?" Adrienne said for the hundredth time.

"It's in the Bible," I said.

"In the Bible? Really? Jesus is going to take people up into the clouds?"

"He's going to suck 'em up like that." Boo snapped his fingers. "Two men will be out working in the field and without any warning atall one of them will just disappear—the Rapture."

"Your father's going to talk about this?" Adrienne asked.

"This morning in church." Grace nodded and took hold of Boo's hand.

"I haven't been inside a church in years, but I think I'll go today. What time is the service?"

"Ten," I said. "I'll save you a seat so you won't feel—you know, funny."

8

The church was hot and airless when we arrived. Both sets of doors were propped open to let in any outside breezes that might blow our way, but there weren't any. Folks were filing into the pews and pulling out the old straw fans before they even sat down. My fan had been eaten away some, probably by one of the Dooley babies, but unfortunately I could still read the tired old ad on the back: Thomson's Funeral Home—May Your Loved Ones Pass the Thomson Way.

I settled in next to Grace and Boo in the front pew, where Daddy liked us to sit, and set to fanning myself.

"Could you turn a little so that's not blowing my way, Charity? I might catch cold."

I glared at Boo. "Just what exactly is this disease you were born with, anyway?" I said. "I mean, how could anyone sit here on a day like today and think it's cold?"

Boo just pulled out his hymnal, set it in his lap, and stared at it.

I looked at his bald head and his small hands gripping the edge of his book and got myself a bad case of the guilts. Of all places to attack someone. I gave him a nudge. "You look real handsome, Boo."

He kept his head down, but I could see a bit of a smile peeking out.

Sharalee gave me a shove from behind as she and her parents took up their fans and sat down behind us. Then in puffed Miss Tuney Mae Jenkins, with her hair dyed cotton-candy pink and her chiffon dress in shades of red billowing about her like clouds in a sunset. Her shoes were covered in a pair of men's black dress socks that she wore on Sundays so she could feel those foot-pedal things on the organ. She was the church organist.

She dropped herself down on the organ bench and began playing some sorrowful tune. Her playing was always a sign for folks to start talking, and I could hear words like

"Rapture" and "Jesus chair" and "phony" weaving in and out of people's conversations while I tried to talk with Sharalee.

"I knew it. I just knew you wouldn't wear that outfit." Sharalee turned to her mama. "Didn't I say she wouldn't wear it? And all that work I put into it! Really, Charity, you should have worn it."

"Sharalee," I said, "just hush, all right? Just hush."

"Oh, I get it. You did wear it, but your daddy made you take it off. What did he say?"

Before I could answer, Mr. Day, Boo's father, leaned forward over the back of the Marshalls' pew and said, "Miss Becky's gone. Miss Anna came by our house this morning after talking with Able. She's just beside herself with worry. Her sister's just disappeared."

"The Rapture!" Boo said.

Grace and Boo gave each other this big-eyed, spooked-out look.

After Mr. Day dropped his little bomb, Mrs. Marshall sidled out of her pew and into another one. The waggin' mouth of the South had work to do.

By the time the choir shuffled across the front of the church, with the women all shouldering their purses like mules lugging saddlebags across the desert, the whole church was talking Rapture. Miss Tuney Mae's organ playing got real soft and she was leaning way off the bench so she could hear what folks were saying, even though I could tell by the know-it-all look on her face that she had already heard, probably from Daddy, which meant that the choir knew, too.

Grace and Boo were holding hands and leaning back in the pew. They were staring up at the ceiling like they figured any minute they would be the next to go.

I was keeping a lookout for Adrienne and was starting to get worried. In a way I was hoping she wouldn't show. I knew Daddy wasn't going to be in the best mood about all this Rapture talk and Jesus chair stuff, but just as Miss Tuney Mae played her last note, in she walked.

She was wearing a fantastic pair of silky flowing pants and some sleeveless flowing top and a big, big straw hat. Looking the way she did, and coming in after the organ, made it seem almost as if she had timed it for a grand entrance. The whole congregation went dead quiet. She stood in the back of the church and looked over all the faces staring at her, then turned her head left, then right. She was looking for something. Then I realized that something was me, and I knew I had to stand up and wave, maybe even call out, if she was going to see me.

I didn't want to stand up and have everybody look at me. I was afraid Daddy would catch me.

I saw the door open at the front of the church, and then in glided Daddy. He stopped as soon as he saw what was going on in the back. I sank lower into my seat, praying Adrienne hadn't caught sight of me, but then my conscience had to go and quote Scripture at me, saying, "But whoever disowns me before men, I will disown him before my Father in heaven."

I thought about how the apostle Peter denied knowing Jesus just before Christ was forced to haul his heavy cross up Calvary Hill. I couldn't live with myself if I thought I would have been one of the people who betrayed Jesus way back then, and wasn't this the same thing? If I betrayed Adrienne, wouldn't it be like I was denying that she saw Jesus?

I gave my father a quick look and saw that he was still looking at the back of the church, so I stood up and waved. Adrienne didn't see me. She was making her way down the aisle, and as she passed the pews, folks were reaching out and touching her, her shoulder or her wrist or a piece of her silk pants, as if she were Jesus Himself making His triumphal entry into Jerusalem. Some of the folks were even whispering things to her, but I couldn't tell what until I heard Mr. Day behind me asking her to pray for his son, Boo. Then Mrs. Marshall lunged forward, reaching out over Sharalee and Mr. Marshall and grabbing Adrienne's hand. "Pray for my Sharalee," she said. "Pray that she loses her weight." Adrienne nodded and smiled, but her shoulders were all hiked up, her face was all white, and her mouth fell back into this skinny straight line with her lips pressed hard as if she were trying to keep a fly from buzzing in. That's when I wondered if she regretted ever having seen Jesus. Was it worth that time of wonderfulness to have to put up with everybody grabbing at you?

I said her name, and when she turned toward me and saw who it was, her shoulders relaxed and she really smiled.

I held out a fan to her. She took it and sat down next to me. Then she leaned toward me and whispered, "I know I'm late. People kept stopping by wanting to see the chair."

Miss Tuney Mae started playing her intro

to "Now to Heaven Our Prayer Ascending," and Daddy, looking all hot in the face like he had already delivered his sermon, strode across the front of the sanctuary and stopped directly in front of me and Adrienne. Adrienne gave my hand a squeeze, and then we all stood up to sing.

Daddy sang the first line real loud and looked straight at Adrienne. His one eyebrow was raised, making him look strict and disapproving. I glanced sideways at Adrienne, but all I saw was straw hat.

The whole time we were singing, Daddy was giving me and Adrienne the hairy eyeball, and when we sang the line in the fourth verse "Every foe at length subduing, God speed the right," Daddy raised his head up and then looked way down at just Adrienne through his glasses, and it was as if he was trying to warn her, or challenge her, or something.

The whole thing made me go all shivery, and when we sat down I snuggled in next to Boo real good and kept my fan on my lap.

The rest of the service went as usual until we came to the sermon, which, for a change, everybody seemed to be looking forward to. There were all kinds of rustlings and settlings-ins going on behind me as Daddy took off his glasses and said a quick prayer about the coming sermon. Then he began by reading from the Book of Jeremiah, and right away the atmosphere changed. It was just like that calm-before-the-storm thing. It was as if the sky had gone all greenish black and the earth was standing still, tense, just waiting for all that electricity to start zinging around.

Daddy began, "This is what the Lord Almighty says: 'Do not listen to what the prophets are prophesying to you; they fill you with false hopes. They speak visions from their *own* minds, *not* from the mouth of the Lord.' "

9

"Are you *ready*—for the *hand*—of *God?*" Daddy shouted down at us from his pulpit.

"Are you?" He glared at the folks on his left.

"Are you?" He glared at the folks on his right.

"Are *you?*" He pointed at Adrienne for a good twenty seconds, saying nothing more.

Then he pushed his glasses up higher on his nose and glared out at the whole congregation.

"We have here today a visitor. A visitor who has *claimed* she has *seen*—Jesus. A *sinner* who has claimed Jesus has come to her! To *her!*

"And this town can hardly control itself. Right away we all *believe*. Right away we're talking Rapture.

"Rapture!

"Let us look at what the Bible says about the Rapture. In the Book of Matthew, Jesus' disciples ask Him *directly*—saying in chapter twenty-four, verse three, 'Tell us,' they said, 'when will this happen, and what will be the sign of Your coming and of the end of the age?'

"And what did Jesus say to them? What was the *first* thing Jesus said to them? He said, 'Watch out that no one deceives you. For many will come in My name claiming, I am the Christ, and will deceive many.'

"*Watch out*—he says. Watch out that no one *deceives* you!

"Yes. Whenever we start looking for signs of Christ's coming we are easily *deceived* by false prophets. And here we have before us today just such a prophet tricking folks with signs of spiritual power and authority. Do not be *fooled* by this sinner, this Antichrist!"

Daddy paused in his shouting and wiped his forehead with a handkerchief. I took the time to glance at Adrienne and saw her sitting as straight and stiff as a deacon's bench. She was clutching her fan and glaring straight at Daddy, not blinking.

Daddy glanced down at his notes and, after a quick feel of his hairpiece, started again, only quieter, whispering almost.

"When we have a false prophet bearing false witness, teaching loose morals, gathering followers to her, we see the breeding of a disease that eats away at the fiber of this church and our families, until there is *total* destruction." His voice started to get louder again. "No longer are we *focused* on *Christ.* No longer do we seek to *love* our neighbor, to *love God.*

"Do not look for special signs. *Look* at Christ.

"Already you people are charging over to Miss Dabney's house. Yes, I know all about it. Already you are worshiping what you believe is an *image* of Christ. A *chair!*

"The Bible tells us that the Antichrist will set up an image of himself and order everyone to worship it. This is an abomination, a mockery! My brothers and sisters, if you have to be *told* it is Jesus who has come, *it—is—not—He!*"

Daddy pounded out the last four words,

his fist beating the Bible lying open in front of him.

"This is *not* the Rapture. Jesus Christ is no closer to you in Miss Dabney's house than He is anywhere else. If you want to communicate with the *Lord*, you must do so in prayer and deed! Would Christ choose a prophet who lives in *sin* with her lover?"

"No. Praise the Lord!" came the voices behind me.

"Would Christ choose a prophet who knows *nothing* of His ways?"

"No, Lord, no! Praise the Lord!" Again the voices, and I wanted to join them. Daddy was right.

But then I got a peek at Adrienne again, her face a picture of shock and disbelief, and I didn't know anymore.

"Matthew twenty-four, verses fifteen through nineteen, says, 'So when you see standing in the holy place, the abomination that causes desolation, spoken of through the prophet Daniel—let the reader understand—then let those who are in Judea flee to the mountains. Let no one on the roof of his house go down to take anything out of the house. Let no one in the field go back to get his cloak.' "

Daddy looked up from his Bible and leaned forward over the pulpit.

"Therefore, I say to you, brothers and sisters assembled here today, when Miss Adrienne Dabney *proclaims* that Christ has come and is waiting for you in her living room, *flee!* Flee to the mountains!"

The voices behind me called out, "Amen!"

"I ask you, if the Rapture *is* at hand, if the *Lord* is about to reach down from the sky and pluck the faithful up to the heavens, will *you* be chosen? Have you done good works here on earth? Have you loved God with *all* your heart, with *all* your mind, and with *all* your body? For surely it is more important for us to be ready, anytime, anywhere, than it is to know *when* the Rapture will happen. It is he who endures to the end who will be saved.

"Are you *ready*—for the *hand*—of God?"

Daddy pulled back from the pulpit and lifted his arms. " 'May our Lord Jesus Christ Himself and God our Father, who loved us and by His grace gave us eternal encouragement and good hope, encourage your hearts and strengthen you in every good deed and word.' Amen, and Amen."

"Amen, praise the Lord!" we all shouted.

Miss Tuney Mae began the intro for the closing hymn and I could hear all kinds of shuffling going on around me. Then, just as we were about to stand up and sing, Adrienne sprang from her seat and without slipping on her sandals rushed up the three steps leading to the pulpit. She turned around to face us and held up her hands. "Wait!" she said.

I saw those dirty bare feet and I felt my face go all hot.

Miss Tuney Mae stopped playing and looked to Daddy to see what she should do. Daddy stepped forward and took ahold of Adrienne's elbow. "Now is not the time for speeches. This is a Sunday-morning worship service, not an open forum."

"I understand that, Able, but you have judged me and judged my motives, and I think it is only fair that I have a chance to defend myself, even if this is a worship service." Adrienne wriggled away from Daddy, crossed her arms, and stood with her feet spread a good two feet apart, looking like she was preparing to have a sit-in or something if he wouldn't let her talk.

"You had your say yesterday," Daddy said, more to the congregation than to Adrienne.

"Aw, let the girlie talk, Able," Old Higgs said.

"Did you not listen to what I said?"

Daddy's eyes practically bulged out through his glasses.

Then from the back of the church came a voice, scratchy but strong. I turned around, and so did everyone else. There, still sober and still in his muddy gardening pants, stood Mad Joe.

"Proverbs three, verses twenty-nine and thirty," he said. Then he paused and nodded to a couple of folks sitting in the back. " 'Do not plot harm against your neighbor who lives trustfully near you. Do not accuse a man for no reason when he has done you no harm.' "

Everyone turned back to Daddy to see what he would do next, and I swanee it was like we were watching a tennis volley—only, before Daddy could react, Adrienne started talking.

"Look, I didn't come here to your town, my mother's hometown, and my birthplace, to stir up any trouble. I came here for my art. My art, and that's all."

Adrienne lifted her chin at us, defying anyone to say that that wasn't why she came. No one said anything. I don't think anyone was even breathing. I know I wasn't.

"I told you people about what I saw because I felt I had to. Yesterday I told you that after it happened, after the visions, I wondered why it had happened and how I was supposed to change and what I was supposed to do about it. Well, the only clear message I've had is that I'm to tell you about it." Adrienne stared off into one corner of the room. "I felt such joy after the first two visions. I felt at peace and contented, and I thought these were my own personal visions. Something I would keep to myself." She looked back down at us. "But then I had the third vision, and I knew that you all had to be told. It wasn't like the other two. It's almost as if Jesus were showing me in stages what it is He wanted to say to me, to all of us. That first vision was just this feeling, this seeing and knowing, more than I've ever known anything, that God is love, pure love, pure light."

"Amen! Hallelujah! Praise the Lord!" Folks were shouting all around me.

"Then, in the second vision, I saw the whole world at once in just a split second. I saw it without seeing." Adrienne flapped her arms down at her sides and shook her head. "I know I'm not making any sense. I don't know—I haven't the right words—there are no words for what I saw and how it happened.

It's as if I didn't see anything, but in my mind somehow I have an image of what I did see. There it was, the whole world, in darkness and in light, and I saw that the love that Jesus showed me before covered all the earth, all of it, every corner, every person."

"Hallelujah! Praise the Lord!"

"And this love—" She closed her eyes and held her face toward the ceiling. "This love is so great and so strong and so perfect that nothing, *nothing* that we feel comes anywhere close to the love Christ showed me He has for this world."

"Hallelujah, yes sir, praise the Lord!" I recognized Mad Joe's voice.

"And I knew all this, I saw all this, and felt it all in a flash of light, in the merest fraction of a second." Adrienne opened her eyes and there were tears in them. She held out her hands toward us as though she wanted to touch us and hold us, maybe rock us in her arms.

She dropped her arms to her sides. "Then I had the third vision. Again, I didn't know what I saw until after I had seen and the images were there in my mind, clear as day.

"I saw this place, this town, and as before, it was covered in the light and love of God. It was Casper. I knew it was Casper. I don't know how I knew. I didn't see the welcome sign, or the Dooleys' store, or this church, or the train tracks—I just knew. And I knew there were people. All of you people were there, and it was good. I felt warm and safe. But then I noticed this black spot in one corner of the town. This one black spot, and it began to spread, growing bigger and darker. It spread and spread until it covered the whole view, until the whole town was in darkness. And I knew this darkness was like a blackened soul, cold and evil."

"Lord have mercy!"

"Then there was this crack of light coming from a break in the ground. The ground was splitting open and this light coming from below was burning away the edges of darkness like it was a piece of charred paper. Only it wasn't a good light, it wasn't God's light. It was light being tossed by the flames that reached up from the ground, and like a thousand fiery fingers it caught hold of someone's leg and pulled that someone under. Then the ground closed up and the flames went away and the light of God seeped back over the town, and I could see Casper again, all lit up except for one spot that remained dark and cold."

I heard Mad Joe call out like he was in

some kind of pain, and I turned to see that he had fallen to his knees and, with his hands together in prayer, he was holding his face up to the ceiling.

"It all happened in a flash," Adrienne said.

I turned back around and caught sight of Daddy still standing next to the pulpit, his fearsome expression looking like it had been freeze-dried on his face.

Adrienne looked over at Daddy. "Now, I've had my say. I've done what I was supposed to do. You can call me a liar, or the Antichrist, or whatever you want. I've said what I believe I was supposed to say."

She stepped down from the altar, but instead of joining me, she strode barefoot down the aisle, her frizzy head held high.

Mad Joe was still at the back of the church, frozen in a state of prayerfulness.

Then Boo jumped up from his seat and turned toward Adrienne's retreating back. "It's me! That somebody in the clutches of the flames of hell is me! Dear *Lord!*"

Adrienne stopped and turned to face him with this look of surprise.

"It's because of the okra," he wailed. "It's because I don't like one of God's gifts and I refuse my okra when there are so many starving people in the world."

Mr. Day stood up and leaned forward over the pew in front of him. "Shh, Boo. God wouldn't—"

Boo shouted over his father's words. "I told Mama that that slimy stuff inside the okra was God spitting saliva, and that He was wrapping it up in his long, green, hairy snot, and sending it down to earth as food. Dear Lord, don't take me! Forgive me. I love okra. I *love* okra! It is Your precious gift of food."

Then Old Higgs stood up and started in right on top of Boo's wailing. I saw Daddy trying to say something, but Old Higgs was determined to out-shout him. Daddy took a few steps back so that he was behind the pulpit. He gripped at its edges and bent his head forward over his Bible and listened to Old Higgs's confession.

"Dear Lord, forgive me. I know it's me You're sending to burn in hell's fiery blaze. I'm the mystery person responsible for the Macy dog incident. And I knew he weren't no rabbit when I shot his leg off, neither, but—shoot!—he was gitting after my chickens like they were . . . Well, anyways, dear Lord, forgive me my sins."

Old Higgs started moaning then, and Daddy tried again to speak, striding back and forth across the platform and shouting about false prophets and the Antichrist.

But then Miss Tuney Mae crashed her fingers down on the organ and played a couple of ear-banging chords. Her head popped up from behind the instrument and she called out, "Lord have mercy upon my soul! I know Satan has come to take me for spreading untruths about folks in my family and this here town. Lord, I am ready for death; but, Lord, make my stay in the underworld a short one, for You have created me as one of Your children who cannot tolerate heat for long periods of time. Forgive me, Lord, all my sins!"

Daddy was shouting out his sermon again. He stood at the edge of the platform, his arms jerking out in front of him, trying to make his point. Spit was flying out of his mouth, but folks were getting hysterical with guilt, and the shouting and confessions rose up out of their mouths, one on top of the other, like a rush of angry waves thrashing their sins and secrets against the shore.

Then came a real surprise. Sharalee stood up behind me with her face just running with tears, and she grabbed hold of my shoulders and started her wailing.

"Lord, I know it's me you're looking for. I have coveted what my best friend has. I have cursed You for making her skinny, all excepting her toes, and for making me so fat and for giving me a skinny mama who hates me. I'm ready, Lord, 'cause it seems to me I'm already burning right here on earth."

Sharalee's fingernails were digging into my bare shoulders and I could feel her warm tears dropping onto my skin.

"Lord, I am ready. I have been evil in my thoughts. I have hated my best friend and cursed You and I've not honored my mother and I eat too much."

Sharalee let go of my back and threw herself all hysterical into her mama's lap.

Daddy had finished spitting out bits of his sermon and was now shouting something about confession being good for the soul, but—and again his words were lost in more hysterical confessions and wailings and the gnashing of teeth.

It wasn't until folks were getting worn out with their sins and things started to quiet down that we heard this tiny pinging tune. Everybody hushed to listen. It sounded like a little toy organ and everybody looked to Miss Tuney Mae to see if she was making the music, but I knew they wouldn't find it there.

I looked down, noticing for the first time what socks I'd put on during my screaming fit, a pair of the Christmas socks Mama had bought.

I stood and held my foot up to Daddy, feeling sure my face was as red as the socks.

"They won't turn off," I said. Daddy was standing there with his face an explosion of purple fury.

"Sorry." I lowered my foot and tried clunking my ankles together, hoping that would stop the tune, but it didn't.

Then Miss Ivy-June, never one to miss an opportunity to sing a solo, stood up in the choir loft and started singing along with the socks, and pretty soon the whole choir was singing, and finally the whole congregation. Everybody sang "We Wish You a Merry Christmas"—everyone, that is, except Daddy— and me.

10

Things happened so fast after we got home from church that Sunday, we didn't have time to eat our dinner. The county sheriff came by saying he needed Daddy to help organize a search party for Miss Becky and someone needed to tend to Miss Anna, who was galloping around town making such a nuisance of herself he was thinking of hauling her into jail until Miss Becky was found.

We got in the car and Daddy started backing it out of the driveway, hoping to follow the sheriff, when in drove Mr. and Mrs. Day, hooting and waving. Mrs. Day jumped out of her car before it even came to a complete stop.

"You need to have a talk with that son of ours, Able," she said. "Miss Dabney's got him so turned around we don't know what we're going to do."

Daddy leaned his head out of the car window. "What's the problem, Corrine?"

"That Boo is setting out on the porch with a suitcase, all ready to go," said Mr. Day, who had gotten out of the car and joined his wife.

"He's running away?" Daddy asked.

"I don't know if he's waiting for those fiery fingers from hell or for Jesus to suck him up into the clouds," Mrs. Day said, "but I do know he's setting out there on the porch with a suitcase full of clean underwear and okra, like they're some kind of passport into heaven."

"Says he won't come back in 'less they find Miss Becky, which he don't think is likely since he knows she's been raptured," added Mr. Day.

Daddy was about to reply to this when we all heard Mrs. Marshall yoo-hooing from behind some bushes over near the graveyard, which was where the shortcut leading to their house was.

"Able, don't you take off till I've had a

word with you, now, you hear?" Mrs. Marshall came marching out from behind those bushes with this fearsome onward-Christian-soldiers look in her eyes.

"You had better have a word with that Mad Joe, or I'm not saying what," she said, storming her way across our drive and tramping down the red dirt like it was Mad Joe under her feet.

"I've just seen those two daughters of his and they're half-dead, sure as I'm standing here. Now, what you going to do about it?"

Daddy was about to say something, 'cause I saw him open his mouth and take a breath, but then Mrs. Marshall started in again.

"It's child abuse, plain and simple. Child abuse. Those girls need doctoring, bless their hearts. No amount of praying's going to cure that anemia disease they got. They need doctoring, sure as certain, and no drunken interference from that worthless father of theirs."

Daddy held his hand out the window like he was signaling a stop and jumped into her stream of talking, saying, "Now hold on, hold on. Mad Joe's had those girls in and out of the hospital, and it's never done a bit of good."

"Pah! That drunken fool. That's just him saying that. Says he doesn't want the hospital interfering with what's between him and the Lord. Interfering! They look yellow! *Yellow!* Like some kind of melon. I promise you, if we don't do something, those two are going to die and we'll all be guilty of murder."

Daddy wrapped his hands back around the steering wheel like he was wishing it was Mrs. Marshall's neck. "All right. Now listen, everybody." He looked up at the Days. "I'll go have a talk with Boo sometime today, but the smartest thing we could do is find Miss Becky, which is what I was just on my way to do."

Then he turned to Mrs. Marshall. "I'll also go have a word with Mad Joe, but you know even if he does take Vonnie and Velita to a doctor again, the doctor won't be able to cure them. Sickle-cell anemia isn't curable."

"Well, they could have their lives extended beyond puberty, I know that. And they'd be a heap more comfortable with medicine. They look like death, you just go see if they don't. Oh, and if you're wanting to find Mad Joe, check out Miss Dabney's. He's over there waiting on line with the rest of the crazies wanting a pray with that chair."

It was at least another ten minutes before the driveway was cleared of people and cars and Daddy could pull out into the road. The first thing he did was drive straight on over to Adrienne's house and round up the folks waiting outside for their turns at the chair, which was easy enough to do once folks heard there was a search party starting up at the Cobb place. The way a couple of the men patted their gun racks and hopped into their trucks, a body would think they were going to hunt down a criminal instead of Miss Becky.

We spent that whole afternoon and evening searching the woods behind the Cobb house and driving around town and hollering out our windows, but we never found her.

The next day Miss Ivy-June's nephew Carl took his crop-dusting plane up for a fly over all the cornfields. The way most of our cornfields were laid out, kind of maze fashion, with no straight line leading you out the other end, it would be easy to get lost in one of them; but Carl landed his plane and climbed down shaking his head. Miss Becky was still missing.

The only good thing about her disappearance was that it kept Daddy so busy he didn't have time to stew over Sunday's Hellfire Incident, as folks were calling it. Every day me and Grace would sit beside Daddy in the car and we'd ride around town looking for Miss

Becky and then calling on Miss Anna to see how she was holding up; and I knew if Mama were home she'd be the one sitting next to Daddy making house calls, and I'd be free to visit with Adrienne. Of course, every day we had to pass Adrienne Dabney's place several times on our way to this and that, and each time Daddy would have to pull off to the side of the road and shake his head at all the cars and trucks parked out front.

On Tuesday morning there were nine of them lined up along the edge of the road, and Daddy said as how this whole town likely as not was going to hell on account of it. On Wednesday there were only three cars parked outside, and Daddy said as how folks were starting to see the light and pretty soon things would be back to normal and maybe there was hope for his flock after all.

For my part, I just kept hoping I'd catch a look at Adrienne, maybe setting in the shade painting some picture or tending to her lawn, but I never did. Then on Thursday afternoon Daddy had to go to a long preachers' meeting over in Eufala, so he said Grace could go visit Boo, who was still out on his porch, and I could stay with Sharalee until he got back. He didn't say I *had* to stay with Sharalee, he just said I could, so I didn't figure it was really dishonest that I went to Adrienne's instead. By then I was wanting to see her extra bad—talk to her, watch her, learn more what it's like to be her. I thought I might even get a look at that Jesus chair, too, but when I got to her house, a long line of people streamed across the lawn and I knew that soon as I put myself at the end of the line, Daddy would come riding by, spot me like I stood ten feet taller than everybody else, and jerk me on home by the hair on my head. And it didn't matter one bit that he was supposed to be in Eufala.

Adrienne stood in the doorway squinting up at me, looking as if she had just waked up even though it was after noon when I rang her doorbell. I held up my sketchpad and reminded her that she had said she would give me an art lesson after her experiment was over.

"Right now? You want me to give you a lesson now?" Adrienne said, rubbing her hand over her face.

"Uh," was all I could think to say.

"Come on in," she said, sighing and tightening the sash of her kimono. I followed her down the hall, staring at the grass and dirt stains along the bottom of her robe, careful not to step on it and trip her.

She led me into her kitchen and told me

to have a seat while she looked for something to eat. I moved a pile of sheets off one of the chairs and set down, looking around while Adrienne stared into the refrigerator. Her sink was stacked with dirty dishes, something Daddy wouldn't allow in a million years, what with dirt and evilness being practically the same thing, and her countertops were covered with packages and boxes of food like she just couldn't be bothered to set them in the cabinets, which I guess she couldn't.

Adrienne let out a laugh and slammed the refrigerator door. "I know what's for breakfast," she said, opening up the freezer. She pulled out a half-gallon carton of chocolate-chip ice cream, grabbed a couple of spoons out of her dishwasher, and joined me at the table.

"Here you go," she said, handing me one of the spoons. It was a big serving spoon, the kind Mama used to serve mashed potatoes. Then she opened the lid of the ice-cream carton and said, "Dig in." And I did! I ate ice cream, right out of the carton, before I'd even eaten my lunch! And we talked about her experiment some, and she said how colors seemed so much more vivid and rich since coming out, and how she noticed everything now—every little thing—and how even a rusty old nail looked beautiful to her.

I tried to get her to talk about the Jesus chair some, but she just kept on talking about art and colors and blades of grass, like art and Jesus were somehow the same thing. Then I dropped a clump of ice cream on her kitchen table and she laughed, and then I laughed, and then we both laughed, and I thought there could be nothing more joyful than eating ice cream straight from the carton, before lunch, with the most splendid person on earth.

After we ate she took me up to her studio, using the back staircase so we wouldn't bother the folks at the Jesus chair, which I wouldn't have minded doing atall. I was just dying to see that chair, but then I saw her studio and I had to stand and marvel at the clutter and the paint and turpentine smell of that real artist's room.

"Wow!" I said, looking at the stacks of wooden frames leaning against the walls and the paintbrushes of every shape and size setting in jars next to a mess of paint tubes and Mason jars filled with brown-red liquid.

"I'm doing most of my painting outdoors," Adrienne said to me, kicking through a pile of her clothes and shoes and such and picking out a skirt and top from off the floor. "But this is a pretty nice studio. The light's good, now that I have the boards off the windows." She chuckled, and then, without any warning atall, she just took off her kimono right there in front of me. She just slipped it off easy as you please so that she was standing in nothing but a pair of underpants and acting like it was just as natural as could be when I knew it wasn't. Even me and Sharalee never got full undressed in front of one another. Most we ever did was get dressed back to back or come out of the bathroom still zipping up our shorts and such.

Adrienne kept on talking about art while she slipped on her top and stepped into her skirt and I nodded and tried to act natural even though I thought my head might just nod right off my neck.

She was talking to me about the kinds of material she painted on, like ragboard, and canvas, and portrait linen, and gessoed Masonite. And I stared at a blank canvas she had leaning against a stack of books, nodding some more and listening real hard.

She told me how each type of material gave a different quality to her work and how which ones she used depended on the scenery, the mood, and the emotion she was wanting to convey. Same with the paintbrushes, she said, and the colors, and whether they were oil or watercolor; all these things made a difference in a painting.

Finally Adrienne was dressed and she sat herself up on a stool and told me I could look through some of her boxes and crates and such, so I did, sticking my head way down into the first box I came to, knowing I was still blushing. I pulled out all kinds of stuff like Turpenoid, and a palette knife, and rabbit-skin glue, and powdered gesso. I found some of her old thumbnail sketches, which were just practice pieces—but they were better than any art I'd ever seen before, except in books, and I realized there was more to this being an artist than I'd thought. I was glad I left my sketchpad downstairs in her kitchen, and I prayed she wouldn't ask to see any of my drawings, which she didn't. Instead she said, "Tell me about yourself, Charity"—which was even worse 'cause that made me stop and think, and what I thought was, there was never a more dull person in all the world than Charity Pittman of Casper, Alabama.

It seemed like forever before I could think up anything to say and then when I did, I just told about my family. I said, "Well, you know about Daddy and him being the preacher and all, and you met Grace."

Adrienne nodded.

"I guess you know she's my younger sister," I said. "Eight years old, and she likes crawling around in dirt and under bushes and really I think she wishes she had been born a bug."

Adrienne laughed as if I had said something clever, which I hadn't, 'cause it was just the truth about Grace, but Adrienne said I was a real delight and she was glad I had come over. That made me want to think up more delightful things to say and so of course my mind went completely blank.

Then Adrienne asked about Mama and I had to go stick my face deep into another box 'cause I didn't know what to say about Mama.

"I heard she collects birdcages," Adrienne said, trying to encourage me, I guess.

"Yes, ma'am," I said, still peering into one of her boxes.

"That's an interesting hobby."

I lifted my head and nodded. "She's even made a few birdcages herself and painted them up real pretty. I've got one of them in my bedroom. She learned how last year at the annual Birdcage Collectors' Convention. That's where she is now, at one of those conventions."

"Really?" Adrienne tilted her head and

looked out the window like she was wondering about something. Like she was wondering about Mama and why she had been gone so long.

I could feel myself blushing all hot again. "Well, she *was* at the convention," I said, "but now she's with my Aunt Nooney in Nashville, Tennessee, visiting cousins."

"Ah," Adrienne said, nodding and turning her head toward me again. "She sounds as if she's a lot like you."

"No. No, we're real different. Mama's not really artistic at all. Those birdcages she made weren't really all that good. Daddy wouldn't even let her set them in any of the formal rooms in the house—that's why me and Grace have them, and—and she's real quiet and . . ."

"And she's flown the coop!" Adrienne hopped off her stool, grinning and nodding like she'd just made some big discovery. "She's off spreading her wings, isn't she? And good for her. Your mother's—"

I jumped up. "No, really, Mama likes cooking and cleaning and singing in the choir. We're not alike atall. She likes going visiting with Daddy, and talking with folks and making them feel good, and—"

Adrienne held up her hand. "Okay, okay. You're right. I've never even met the woman. Anyway"—Adrienne turned away from me real quick, bent over a pile of stuff, and dug out a muddy-looking sketchpad—"I promised to give you an art lesson, so come on, let's see some of your drawings."

11

Adrienne's art lesson made me forget all about what she said about Mama. I learned more in her one hour of teaching me than I'd ever learned about anything. She showed me a whole new way of seeing. She told me I was drawing what I thought a rose should look like rather than the rose I was seeing. She showed me how to look at lines and shapes and negative spaces instead of seeing only flowers and trees, and I understood, and law if I didn't draw the most real-looking hat right there in front of her. It was her hat, the straw one she wore in church that past Sunday. I was thrilled right down to my toenails that she let me draw it, and when I hurried on home, hoping to get there before Daddy came back, I knew I was hurrying with a memory from her tucked under my arm.

When I got up to my room, I tore the drawing out of my sketchpad, stuck it into the edges of my mirror, and removed Mama's birdcage off the chest of drawers so I could have a clear view of Adrienne's hat while lying right there on my bed. And every time I looked at it, which was often, I would think on Adrienne and all her exciting ways.

The next day was Friday, and still Miss Becky was missing. Daddy couldn't go looking for her that day 'cause it was his turn to be the visiting chaplain at the Flowers Hospital in Dothan. He told Grace that she could go stay with Boo again, and I was hopeful that I'd get another afternoon with Adrienne; but he told me I was old enough to go with him, and so that whole day I watched my daddy say prayers with the sick and fearful, and hold their hands, and hug them when they cried, and I was so proud. I was proud to be his daughter, proud that he cared about people so much, and proud that he believed so strongly in God and the Bible and such. It was a joy in my heart to know he was a good man, a real good man.

We were so full of good feelings for one another, the way it used to be before the summer, before Mama left and Adrienne came to town, that driving back home that day I didn't even think about searching out Adrienne when we drove past her house. Shoot, I wasn't even looking at that side of the road; but Daddy was, and he said, "What in the—" and I felt the car speed up and then stop short, and when I turned my head to look, I saw the picnic all over again. There were cars and trucks everywhere—on the lawn, across the street, in the driveway—and gathering out in front of the house looked to be the whole town of Casper.

Miss Tuney Mae Jenkins pulled her old Fleetwood up behind us and shouted, "Hey, y'all, come get me out of this contraption." I started to get out of the car to go help, but Daddy pulled me back.

"I'll do it," he said in this barking, snarly kind of voice.

He got out of the car, leaving his door open, and I slid across the seat, climbed out, and followed him. By the time we reached Miss Tuney Mae, Sharalee was already helping her out. When we caught a look at each other, we gave one another this embarrassed look like we were meeting for the first time, and in a way we were. We hadn't seen each other since her confession.

Old Higgs Holkum was leading the line of folks back out toward the cars, back out toward us.

Daddy waited for them with his arms folded across his chest, leaning against Miss Tuney Mae's car and not saying a word. For a change, neither was Miss Tuney Mae.

"Evening, Able, ladies," Old Higgs said when he got close enough to be heard. He gave a glance behind him like he was making sure everyone was still there and then said, "We're having a special prayer meeting tonight and, uh, it would be nice if you were to lead it. It's for Miss Becky, of course."

Daddy gazed out over his congregation, almost as if he were making a list in his head of all the people there that night. Folks were trying to tuck in behind one another, getting out from under Daddy's eyes, but Daddy started walking back and forth, still with his eyes on them, and they couldn't hide, just like they couldn't hide from the Lord.

He finally stopped in front of Old Higgs

again. "You're wanting me to lead you in prayer." He glanced up at the sky and so did I. The clouds hung low and gray-white, like a cluster of cow udders ready for milking.

"It looks like rain, thank the good Lord," Daddy said. "Why don't y'all get in your cars and we'll meet back at the church, where we can stay dry?"

Nobody made a move for their cars. They just stood there, shifting their feet and staring at the ground and digging their hands into their pockets, even if they didn't have any.

"Well, see, it's like this," Old Higgs said, crossing his arms and tucking his hands into his armpits. "We're wanting to do it round Miss Dabney's chair."

Daddy's eyes glared out at them through his glasses. "Are you mad? I would never play a part in such an abomination! If you don't care to do it at the church, then I suggest we say a quick prayer right here, right now." Daddy made this come-let-us-gather-together gesture with his arm, but everybody just stood there watching their feet some more.

"I hate to admit it, Able, but that chair does have a certain glow about it," Hank Dooley said.

Folks lifted their heads and nodded.

"Couldn't hurt any," said Dale Dooley.

Daddy backed up against Miss Tuney Mae's car. "This is outrageous. It's blasphemous. I cannot condone such idolatry."

"Please, Able, for my sister," said Miss Anna.

"For your sister I will pray at home, as I have done all week. Now, if there are those of you who wish to pray with me, please step forward. The rest of you, go! Go to your graven image!"

For a whole minute it seemed nobody moved, or breathed, or anything, and I thought they were going to stay and pray with Daddy; but then Old Higgs turned and walked toward the yellow house, and that started everyone moving back into the line, streaming back toward Adrienne's glowing Jesus chair.

Miss Tuney Mae and Sharalee were the only ones who stayed put.

"It's just that they had this all planned, Able," Miss Tuney Mae said. "It ain't no disrespect to you."

"Sheep! You're all sheep!" he yelled at their backs. "Sheep without a shepherd, and you will follow—you will follow that woman like lambs to the slaughter." He raised his fist in the air. "Mark my words." Then he looked over at me and said, "Charity, get in the car. It's your bedtime."

I hurried to the car, climbed in, and looked down at my watch. It was just ten minutes past six.

12

All week I had been good about not visiting that Jesus chair, but hearing that the chair actually glowed was too much for me. I just had to go see it. I had to be at that prayer meeting, 'cause I just knew there was going to be magic that night.

Problem was, how was I going to get there? Daddy had sent me to my room as soon as we got home, punishing me for sins I didn't even commit.

"It would serve him right if I just snuck out of the house," I told myself. I paced the floor of my room and listened to the rain and thunder overhead. Anyway, I would be doing it for a good cause. I would be helping Miss Becky and Miss Anna. I wouldn't go to hell for that, would I?

Adrienne's vision of the flames pulling someone down into the earth and the earth closing up over him flashed through my mind. I shuddered and started singing, "Lord, I want to be a Christian in-a my soul," trying to block out the thought.

I went to my closet and searched through the pile of junk on the floor for an umbrella, singing all the while. I tossed aside a couple of broken birdcages, found another old drawing pad, and stuffed it into my backpack, just in case Adrienne was at the meeting and wanted to teach me something else about drawing. I dug a little deeper but couldn't find the umbrella.

I went to my bedroom door and opened it. Daddy was in his study yelling at someone on the phone. Maybe with the rain and thunder and all his noise I could tiptoe downstairs, grab an umbrella out of the closet, and sneak out the front door.

I crept out into the hallway, closing my door behind me. Grace opened her door and peeked out. Daddy had sent her to bed early, too. I put my finger to my mouth, signaling her to keep quiet, and she closed her door. "Lordy, what kind of example am I setting for her?" I said under my breath.

I made it to the hall closet and found myself an umbrella. Daddy was still shouting into the phone. I realized he was shouting at Mama. I couldn't help but stop and listen.

"I've got to put an end to this," Daddy said. "They are *my* congregation. The Lord is challenging me and I shall rise to the challenge. I shall not fail. I won't let my flock down. I won't let the Lord down."

He listened and then he said, "What? Of course it matters. They're out of control. They're all skating on the edge of reason, under the influence of that woman. She's brought nothing but sin to this town."

Daddy paused again and then said, "Why are you telling me this? What do you mean? How can you stay another day, knowing what's going on here? Don't you realize our own daughter's bedeviled by this woman?"

There was a long silence and then Daddy put the receiver down.

"Have I lost it?" I heard him ask in this sad voice. "Am I a modern-day Job, losing my family, my congregation—everything? How long shall I be tested?"

"Daddy, I'm here," I whispered. "You haven't lost me." I closed the closet door and leaned against it. I shut my eyes and thought of Adrienne gathering around that glowing Jesus chair with everybody there except me. I could hardly stand the thought.

"What in heaven's name are you doing downstairs?"

I jerked my head sideways and saw Daddy standing at the end of the hallway.

"What is this? What are you doing downstairs?" he asked again. "Were you listening in on my conversation?" He marched down the hall toward me.

"No—I mean, I didn't . . ."

He glared at me, standing before me with his hands on his hips, making the shoulder pads in his jacket puff up. I wanted to back away but I had the closet door pressed against my back.

"And where did you think you were going?" He grabbed the umbrella out of my hands, which until then I had forgotten I was holding.

"No, don't tell me. Let me tell you. You were going to that meeting, weren't you? You were going to sneak out of this house. You git on up those stairs!" Daddy clapped his hands and started chasing me toward the stairs.

I ran, squealing like a greased pig, knowing what was coming. As we got to the stairs he was paddling my behind with every step I took, following me up to my room and then charging ahead of me. He flung my door open and let it slam against the wall.

"You are never to see that Adrienne Dabney again, you hear? Never! Now, you get in your room and stay there. And don't even think of sneaking out again. I'll be watching you. And tomorrow I expect you to memorize twenty Bible verses, starting with all of Leviticus nineteen, which begins in verses three and four with 'Each of you must respect his *mother* and *father*,' and 'Do not turn to idols or make gods of cast metal for yourselves. *I am the Lord your God.*' "

Daddy grabbed the doorknob and slammed the door behind him, leaving me alone in my room to wonder what had just happened.

I waited a bit and then opened my door a crack and peered out. Grace was peering back at me.

13

I was mad at Daddy, really mad. I don't think I'd ever felt that way about him before and it was giving me all kinds of crazy thoughts. I was questioning everything. Like why should I stay away from someone who could help me, who could show me how to be a real artist, a real somebody? And how could Adrienne be of the devil if she saw Jesus setting in her chair and He showed her all that love and such? And especially, why did it seem as if I was getting the blame for everything? What did I do?

That's what decided me going over to

Adrienne's the next morning instead of learning those verses like Daddy wanted. I knew he was going to be in Dothan meeting with some other preacher for a couple of hours, so why shouldn't I go over? Anyways, if I was going to be yelled at all the time and sent to bed while it was still daylight out, then I was going to do something worth the punishment.

As soon as I saw Daddy's car roll out of the driveway, I grabbed my backpack with my sketchpad and Bible in it, drank down a few gulps of milk straight from the carton, and set off for Adrienne's. I caught sight of Grace cutting through a hedge on her way to Boo's and wondered why she got to go anywhere she pleased while I had to be sneaking around if I wanted a life. I put the thought out of my mind and breathed in a lungful of air, sweet smelling after last night's rain. I picked my way around the fields and puddles, feeling braver, more sure of myself the closer I got to Adrienne's.

When I reached the house, I saw Mad Joe's truck and one of his signs, a new one, sinking into the lawn. It said, Jesus Chair Around Back. I decided to follow the sign, getting excited all over again at the thought of finally seeing the chair for myself.

At the back of Adrienne's house, tacked to the porch door, was another sign that said, Wait on the Porch If Room Is Occupied. I stepped inside and saw yet another sign hanging from a string on the entrance door to the living room. It said, Occupied, and was outlined in red. I flipped it over and the other side said, Free, and was outlined in green. I turned it back to Occupied and sat down in a rocking chair and waited.

Finally the door opened, and out stumbled Mad Joe, looking the way I was used to seeing him: unshaven, wearing dusty black pants, a booze-stinking white shirt, and his suspenders, and carrying his shotgun.

"Charity!" He lunged toward me and grabbed ahold of my wrist, the gun clunking up against my thigh.

"Pray for my babies. The Lord has spoken to me. You pray for my babies and believe."

"Yes, sir, I will," I said, standing up and keeping an eye on the gun.

He got up real close in my face and his lips puffed out a breath of stale liquor that curdled the milk slushing around in my stomach.

"Pray for my babies. The Lord said, 'Feed them grain,' and I did. The Lord knows they ain't done nothing wrong." He let go of my arm and straightened up. "No sir. They ain't done nothing. Just like my Datina. You remember my Datina? The Lord can't take my babies away."

"I'll pray for them, Mad Joe."

He patted my arm. "You're a good girl. The Lord won't take good girls. The Lord won't take my babies. You gonna pray for my babies?"

I edged my way toward the open door. "Yes, sir. I'll go do it now. I'm sorry they're sick."

"T'ain't sick no more. I fed them grain and I believe. I believeth in the Lord." Mad Joe lunged toward me again, half-stumbling over the shotgun. I squealed and ran inside the house, closing the door behind me and locking it.

When I turned around, right away I saw the chair. The room was dark 'cause all the curtains were drawn, but the chair stood out from the gloom as if it were glowing. Just like it was glowing. I felt my scalp contract like my hair was getting ready to stand on end. The house was all hushed up quiet except for the fan whirring and blowing on the other side of the room. I figured Adrienne was still asleep. I looked at the chair again, then around the room, and then back at the chair. Mad Joe had left some rosemary on the seat. I knelt down in front of it and closed my eyes.

"Hey, Lord, Jesus Christ, sir," I began, "I don't know if I'm sinning just being here. Daddy would say I am, but how could praying be a sin?

"I'm scared. I have a feeling, just kneeling here, that something's going to happen, something bad. Am I having a vision?" I opened my eyes. Everything was still dark and the chair still glowed, kind of, but nothing else. I kept my eyes open in case a vision was coming, and continued with my prayer. "First off, I pray that Miss Becky is found, 'cause Miss Anna is sick with worry and we've got to get Boo and his rotten okra off his porch. Grace says the okra's staining his underwear. I hope Miss Becky is all right.

"And Mad Joe, he's a good soul really, don't you think? Don't you think his girls should be healthy now? They've been sick forever with that anemia thing, and they're the smartest girls in the whole country . . . so they should stay alive, don't you think?" I waited in case God was planning to use his "still, small voice" on me. I didn't hear anything, so I went on. "Mama's always lecturing me

about letting things happen in God's time—
Your time. Always saying I don't need to push
so hard for things and that if I let go and let
You handle it, it will all turn out just right.
Something, she says, me and Daddy need to
learn. Well, there's lots of things I'm wanting
to have turn out just right, Lord, but the problem with waiting for Your time, dear Lord, is
that it's not measured in minutes or hours, or
even years, but in these eternities, and that's
just too long for me. Forgive me, Lord, but
it is.

"I see how quiet Mama is all the time, and
patient, and then comes the convention and
she just lights up and it's like the whole rest
of the year she's just waiting, collecting her
birdcages and waiting for that birdcage convention to come around again. Lord, is that
how we're supposed to live?"

I looked at the chair and, really, it seemed
to glow brighter. Chills were running up and
down my arms. "And Lord . . . I need to
know . . . Is she coming back? I mean, is she
ever coming back?" I whispered this part so
quiet, afraid that just asking about Mama
would keep her away, but I knew the Lord
heard.

I closed my eyes. "Now about Daddy,
Lord. I know he's like one of your disciples

and he's always right about things, but I know, too, that Adrienne is telling the truth and isn't the Antichrist leading us astray. But how can Daddy and Adrienne both be right?

"I know the answer is something clever like in the Bible when, Lord Jesus, You were accused of healing some sick lady on the Sabbath, which was a wrong thing, and yet You made it right by telling Your accusers that setting her free of her affliction was the same as them setting free their oxen and donkeys so the animals could have water on the Sabbath. It's like that somehow, isn't it, Lord?

"Well, I pray they can get along and that Daddy lets me see Adrienne again and that I become a famous artist. I know, Lord, I said I was going to be a preacher lady. And see, here I am, facing You and telling the truth. I can preach the Word through my art, don't You think? Don't You think there are other ways of being a preacher besides standing behind a pulpit every Sunday? If You do, I wish You'd put that idea in Daddy's head so he could understand, too.

"Well, Lord, forgive me for such a long prayer, but I've been saving it all up so I could bring it here to You, to this chair. I really feel You're here with me."

I sat there another five or ten minutes, I

don't know how long, just staring at the chair, a straightback wooden chair with two slats across the back and a rush seat. Plain, and white, and glowing. And I felt this holiness feeling spread all through me, and I wished that I could carry that feeling around with me all the time. I prayed to Jesus Christ, our Lord, that I could carry that feeling around with me all the time.

14

I knew I had to get up in case someone else was waiting on the porch wanting to use the chair, but I couldn't bring myself to move. Right then I wanted to stay in that house always. I was ready to never set eyes on my daddy or Grace or Mama or anyone again. I was ready to become one of those nuns that hole up somewhere in a cave and float around with this holy smile on their faces, never speaking to anyone but God.

I leaned forward and kissed the chair, just in case Jesus was setting in it in His invisible state, and then I got up and floated over to the door, just knowing I was smiling my own holy smile.

The sun hit me full force when I stepped out onto the porch, but it felt good, like Jesus was shooting these warm love rays into my body. I sat down in the rocker and, with my eyes closed, just rocked and rocked and let myself feel the sun and Jesus and all His love burning through me. Then I reached into my pack and pulled out my Bible, figuring I would learn my verses while that holy feeling was still there.

"Charity?"

I sprang from my chair, thinking I'd heard my daddy. I felt this weight of guilt and fear crushing into my chest like the rock of ages and I couldn't breathe.

"Hey, girl."

I turned around and saw Sharalee through the screen, standing outside wearing this big-hair hairdo.

I let out my breath. "Law, you scared me."

"Sorry." She came onto the porch. "Don't tell Mama I was here, okay?" she said.

I nodded. "Long as you don't tell my daddy on me."

Sharalee giggled. "Well, now, Charity Pittman sneaking from her daddy, I do declare!"

"Just don't say anything, okay?"

"Oh, don't worry about me." Sharalee poofed up her hair with her hand. "I've got better things occupying my mind these days."

"Like what?"

"Like Mama training me for the Miss Peanut pageant," she said. She squinted her eyes at me. "And don't you dare laugh. I've already lost two whole pounds, and that's with eating stuff right in front of Mama, too."

I swallowed. "You look real good, Sharalee, and I like your hair big like that. Makes your face look right skinny."

Sharalee went on like I hadn't even spoken. "Mama says if I can lose twenty-five pounds by next April she'll buy me the best store-bought gown this side of the Mason-Dixon."

"But what if you don't lose the weight? What's she going to do then?"

"I'm going to lose the weight, and she's going to buy me the dress and get me in that pageant, and see if I don't win! Then who'll be laughing at me?"

"Sharalee, I'm not laughing. It's just that, law, twenty-five pounds!"

Sharalee closed her eyes. "I'm going to lose it just the same. Jesus promised."

I glanced at the house. "The Jesus chair? You've asked Jesus to lose that weight for you? And win you that contest?"

"I believe, don't you, Miss Preacher's Daughter?"

"I do. I—yes—yes, I do. Oh, Sharalee." I threw my arms around my very best friend. "I'll pray, too. I'll come here every day and pray for you. That chair works, I'm just sure it does."

Sharalee gave me a squeeze and then let go. "I know it does. They had that prayer meeting last night, finishing up with Miss Ivy-June singing 'His Eye Is on the Sparrow,' and you know, they sang the last amen at ten o'clock exactly, and at exactly ten o'clock a call came into the sheriff's office from some folks in Selma, said they had Miss Becky with them. Now how about that for a miracle?"

"What? They found Miss Becky? Was she kidnapped? She probably set fire to their getaway car, more 'n likely, and they turned her in." I spun around. "They found Miss Becky!"

Sharalee grabbed my arms. "Charity, really," she said. "She wasn't kidnapped. She was just going home. She grew up in Selma. She forgot she lived here, see, and she went back home. She forgot where she lived. The doctors say she's got Alzheimer's disease."

"But they found her, I don't believe it! Does my daddy know? He should have been the first to know. Wait till everybody hears. Boo! Does Boo know? He's free at last! They found her, Sharalee, they found her! Isn't that great?" I grabbed her again and started jumping up and down.

"It's Jesus. It's the chair." Sharalee said, keeping her body still, refusing to be jostled up and down. "And I'm going to lose that weight and become Miss Peanut."

"Yes, you are. Oh, Sharalee, I'm so proud." I gave her another hug, and she held her body stiff.

"I'm serious, Charity," she said in this warning kind of voice.

"Well, sure," I said, backing off.

"No more snacks in the barn and hiding extra in the coffins. I confessed it all to Mama anyway, and to Jesus. I have to do my part if Jesus is going to do His."

"Of course."

"And no telling Mama about me and the chair." Sharalee stared down at the grass. "She fierce doesn't believe in the chair. But I'll show her. We'll show her, me and Jesus."

15

Sharalee went inside for a talk with the Jesus chair, and I set off for home, hoping I'd get there before Daddy got back. I was still in the driveway when I saw Adrienne speeding down the road in her beat-up station wagon. She swerved into her drive and I jumped out of the way. She slammed on the brakes and hopped out of her car laughing. "Did I frighten you?"

"I thought you were inside asleep," I said.

"On a day like this? My God! It's too fantastic. I finished!"

"You finished?"

Adrienne nodded. "I finished my first painting since my sensory deprivation project. Come tell me what you think."

I followed her around to the back of the car, thinking on what I was going to say about her painting. I figured "marvelous" would be good, and maybe "splendid," too.

Adrienne flipped through her set of keys, searching for the right one to unlock the back. I watched her hands. They were darker than her arms or her face, like they hung outside more often than the rest of her. And they were strong and rough looking, nothing like her body, which was tiny and thin and made me feel like some kind of oaf to be standing next to her. She had on a man's oxford-cloth shirt, worn with the sleeves rolled up and paint all over it—and in her hair, always paint in her hair. I loved it. I wanted to look just like her.

Adrienne opened the back and lifted out her painting. It was a large canvas. Her arms were out as far as they would go, just trying to hold on to the sides.

"I painted this out in the fields in back of Mad Joe's little place," she said, holding the canvas up in front of her. "Well, what do you think?" Her eyes were all sparkling.

I stared at the canvas. I didn't know what it was exactly, but I knew how it made me feel. It hinted at trees and water, lots of cool water—maybe—and lots of space in shades of gray and white. It gave me that same feeling I had the time I went with Daddy to the church in Atlanta to hear him preach. The time I decided to become a preacher 'cause I was so full of that holy feeling, the same feeling I had with the Jesus chair. I stared at her painting a long time, not wanting to pull away or even speak for fear of losing that feeling. I no longer saw any trees or water, just shapes and colors that washed over me like a wet spring morning. And, law, I felt that burning desire Adrienne had once talked about. That fierce desire to create something of my own, create my own holy thing.

"You like it, I can tell," Adrienne broke into my thoughts.

I looked up at her and then back at the picture. "It's almost—it's almost holy." I felt my face and body go hot; a squiggle of sweat ran down from my armpit.

"Holy!" she said. "You couldn't have said anything better. You have an artist's eye, Charity, you really do. Have you been practicing your drawing?"

I opened my mouth to answer but Adrienne jumped in, saying, "Oh! We have to celebrate my painting. I always celebrate. Hold on, I'll be right back."

She set her painting back in the car and scooted off toward the house. She was gone less than a minute, and when she came back she carried a full bottle of wine and two glasses in her hands.

"Now to celebrate," she said, lifting the bottle.

"Oh no, I can't." I backed away some. "Daddy'd tar and feather me for sure if I so much as caught a whiff of that devil's poison."

Adrienne laughed and set the bottle and glasses down on the car. "Charity, this isn't hard liquor. In Paris even *les enfants* drink a bit of wine. Now, I feel too fabulous to argue. I'll pour you just a drop, and then we'll say cheers to the completion of my painting and we'll have ensured the painting's success."

I must have nodded or something, 'cause she poured half a glass of the stuff and handed it to me, and Lord have mercy, I took it.

She raised her glass. "To *The Holy*," she said.

"Really?" I said. "You're going to call it *The—*"

Adrienne nodded and said again, "To *The Holy!*"

"To *The Holy!*" I repeated, and clinked my glass against hers. I took a sip and told myself, *Drink this in remembrance of me*, which is what Daddy always said before we drank the grape juice during communion service. I was hoping Jesus, and Daddy, if he ever found out, would count this as a kind of outdoor communion. I even tried to keep my mind on the Last Supper the whole time I was feeling that devil's liquid burning down my throat, but I couldn't help it, part of the time I had this juice and joy feeling rushing all through me 'cause I was picturing myself setting with Adrienne in Paris, sipping wine at an outdoor café.

Adrienne set her glass down empty and picked up the bottle. I set mine down with one sip missing and said a quiet "Amen."

I saw Old Higgs's truck turning into the driveway and I jumped in front of my glass, hoping Old Higgs wouldn't see and tell on me. Adrienne shook her head and said, "You know, Charity, one of these days just pleasing your father won't be enough. You're going to have to please yourself. Free yourself and take off! Be your own person!" Adrienne had poured herself another glass of wine and was letting the stuff just spill down her throat.

Old Higgs climbed out of his truck and came over to us. "Miss Adrienne, Charity," he said, lifting his hat from his head, then setting it back on.

"Hey, Mr. Holkum," I said.

Adrienne poured herself another glass of wine and nodded.

Old Higgs peered around my back, saw the other glass, grinned, and said, "Got a message for your pappy."

I didn't say anything. I just squinted into the sun and waited for him to go on.

"Miss Becky's been found, praise the Lord and hallelujah. We had that prayer meeting, and now she's found. Glory, glory, we got us a miracle. Jesus, praise the Lord, is with us."

"Yes, sir," I said. "I heard about that. I'm real pleased."

"Who's been found?" Adrienne asked, holding out her canvas again and examining it.

"Miss Becky, ma'am," said Old Higgs.

"Is she your dog?"

Old Higgs adjusted his shoulders. "No— you know, we had that prayer meeting at your house last night, praying for her to be found. The old woman who lives with her sister, yonder." Old Higgs pointed out toward the road, although the Cobbs lived about a mile from Adrienne's.

"We was hoping, if it was all right with you, Miss Adrienne, that we could meet again tonight. We got to praise the Lord, give thanks for His blessings."

Adrienne nodded and said, "I've got to go into town and call my dealer." Then she turned and walked off toward the house with her painting, and me and Old Higgs just stood looking at each other, not sure if she'd answered him or not.

"Well," he finally said, "you make sure you tell your pappy, now, you hear?" Then he turned and walked back to his truck.

I stood there for a moment and watched him back out of the drive, the red dirt clouding up around his wheels. Then I set off again myself, full of thoughts about Adrienne and how she had said that someday pleasing my daddy wouldn't be enough; and seeing her painting, seeing her so full of the life I wanted, I knew it already wasn't.

16

I was hurrying along the edge of the corn-fields, sure Daddy had beat me home, when I thought I heard someone whispering my name. I turned this way and that but didn't see anybody. I took a couple more steps and heard it again.

"Charity, here. Up here I am."

I looked up and saw Boo's hairless legs dangling from a branch.

"Boo, what you doing up there? Where's Grace?"

He swung his body around the branch and dropped to the ground.

"I've got to tell you something," he said. He wiped at his nose with his arm.

"I already know Miss Becky's been found. I guess the Lord hasn't need of you after all." I turned to leave and he caught my arm. His hand was cold.

"Say, what are you doing in shorts and short sleeves?" I said, turning back around to face him. "Aren't you supposed to have some kind of cold blood running in you or something?"

Boo waved his hand. "That's just Miss Tuney Mae saying that. I just catch the chill easy, is all—but I'm thinking maybe I been cured since waiting on the porch with the okra and going to see that Jesus chair this morning."

I grabbed his Crimson Tide cap off his head and examined his scalp. "Nope, don't see a single strand of hair yet."

"Oh, you're so smart." Boo wagged his head at me and grabbed his cap back. "That isn't what I was a-going to tell you, anyways. There's some kind of upset going on at your house. I think you'd better get on home."

"Well, where do you think I was headed?" I yelled at him, knowing it was my own fear making me cross. I stomped off, trying to block out Boo's last words.

"It's real bad. The reverend's fit to be tied."

I kept walking—slowly, but I kept walking. I knew it was no good putting off what I knew was coming. I scanned the side of the road for a good switch, found one, and continued walking, whipping the switch in the air and listening to it whistle.

When I got to the house I slowed down even more, dragging my switch behind me. I expected to see Daddy waiting for me on the porch, pacing and jingling his change, but he wasn't there. I entered the house through the kitchen and listened. No sound. I took a couple of steps farther into the kitchen and stopped again. No movement. Where was he? I left the kitchen and stopped in the hallway. I jumped when I saw a dark figure moving at the other end.

"Daddy?"

He was standing in front of the window, the sun behind him so that he looked more like a shadow than a person.

"Charity."

I held up my switch. "I brought me a switch sized to fit the deed."

Daddy walked toward me, saying nothing, showing nothing on his face about what he was thinking. I backed up and he reached forward and set his hands on my shoulders. "The devil has got ahold of this house with his teeth and is shaking it down to its very foundation."

"Yes, sir," I said.

"We must overcome this evil! We must get at the very heart of it and wipe it out today. Today! The devil shall not tear us asunder!" He was shaking me. With each word he was shaking me as though he thought the very heart of this evil thing was living inside of me.

"Daddy, you're scaring me." I wrenched myself free, but Daddy stayed close.

"We will put on the full armor of God so that we can take our stand against the devil's schemes." He glared at me. "Get your sister down here and meet me at the car." Daddy marched toward the front door, then turned around and said, "This instant!"

I ran up to Grace's room and knocked on the door.

"Come in," she called out.

I stepped inside and looked around. It wasn't a room I often went in, and not just because we weren't ones to be talking with each other much. There just wasn't room for Grace and her stuff and anyone else. I don't think she owned a single toy or doll, but she did have the world's largest collection of rocks—most likely all from her head—and birds' nests and arrowheads, and she had all kinds of cacti growing in pots with their long needles poking out just daring you to not look where you were going, and strung up like necklaces across her windows were pinecones. I guess she liked prickly things.

"Daddy wants us in the car this instant," I said. Grace was working on her bird-feather collection. She was kneeling at the side of her bed and taping a few new feathers to a huge square of cardboard.

I went and stood over her.

Grace looked up, her yellow hair sweeping the cardboard.

"Did you hear me?"

"She's not coming back," she said.

"Who? Mama? 'Course she is. She's just staying on extra. What makes you think she's not coming back?"

Grace didn't answer. She had gotten the tape stuck to her fingers and it was twisting and sticking to itself.

"Gracie?"

She frowned. "I heard the reverend on the phone with her, and when he hung up he said, 'She's gone.' "

"Me. I was gone, not Mama. I was supposed to be here at home learning my Bible verses, but I wasn't. It's me he was talking about."

"But—"

"Gracie, put down that stupid tape and listen to me."

Grace pushed off from the bed and stood up. The tape dispenser was dangling from the twisted line of tape still stuck to her fingers.

"It was me who was gone, okay? Not Mama. She'll be back. She'll be back. She always comes back."

I pulled the tape off her fingers and stuck it on the bed.

"Now come on before Daddy has a real fit."

We raced down the stairs and out to the car. Daddy wasn't there. We climbed inside and sat there with the car doors open 'cause of the heat, and waited for Daddy. Then we saw him coming out of the garage, holding an ax in his hands. I jumped out of the car.

"What's that for?" I asked, following him around to the back.

"Get in the car." Daddy opened the trunk, shoved aside some old birdcages, and dropped in the ax.

"But what's that for? What are you fixing to do?"

He slammed down the lid and leaned into the car, his hands pressing against the top of the trunk, his eyes staring into his own reflection.

"Every day I'm hearing the Lord calling me to take up the ax and reduce that chair to splinters, and today I'm going to do it." He pounded the car with his fist. "Yes, in the name of the Lord, I'm going to do it."

"The Jesus chair? You're going to chop up the Jesus chair? But you can't! Daddy, you can't!" I tried to squeeze between him and the trunk, but he grabbed my arms and shook me.

"Oh yes. Indeed I can—I must." He released me. "Now get in the car." He turned away, moving to his side of the car and opening the door.

I grabbed the back of his jacket, pulling it back from his shoulders, and cried, "But it's the Jesus chair. I need it!"

Daddy whirled around, and I heard his jacket tear as it ripped through my fingers.

"It is Satan's chair."

"No! You don't understand!" I cried. "I really need it. How can we ever get Mama ba—"

"Don't you dare say it!" He raised his hand in warning, and I drew back. "It's you who doesn't understand. You're but a child, who thinks and speaks as a child. You don't listen for the Lord as I do. You don't study the prophet Isaiah and know that he says, 'All who make idols are nothing and the things they treasure are worthless.' "

He pointed his finger and then pressed it against my chest, just below my neck. " 'Those who would speak up for them are blind; they are ignorant to their own shame.' Yes, Charity, that is in Isaiah, and he tells us that those who worship idols will be brought down to terror and infamy. To *terror* and *infamy!* Do you understand? You, Adrienne, this whole town brought down by God's wrath."

I stepped back, away from him, not in fear of him but in fear of myself. I couldn't believe what I had done. I had grabbed his jacket and ripped it, I had answered back and hadn't been afraid to do it, and worst of all, there was more I was wanting to say and I knew I was going to say it.

"You—you quote Scripture and it sounds right, Daddy," I began, moving toward him again. "But it feels wrong to destroy the chair." My voice grew louder. "It *is* wrong. I know it. Jesus is there. It would be like chopping up Jesus Christ. You're going to chop up Jesus Christ! Daddy, you can't do it!"

Daddy's face exploded with rage, and I felt the sting of his hand as it smacked against my cheek. "Jesus Christ dwells within us all!" his voice boomed. "He is not a chair! He is not a piece of wood! He's here. In here!" He pounded his chest. "How I have failed you if you can't see that! If this town can't see that . . . You have opened your soul to Satan and he has walked right in. You have no need of the chair. It is the devil who needs it." He pounded the roof of the car.

I looked away and rubbed at my cheek, smearing my tears around on my face. He had never slapped me before. He had never slapped anyone before. I wanted to drop to my knees and curl up into a tight ball and cry out for Mama, but I didn't. I kept talking, and my voice was quiet and tiny when I spoke.

"Isn't it ever just all right to listen to our feelings, Daddy? Aren't our feelings ever right?"

"No, daughter, never. Our feelings alone are never right. Now, I'm telling you, get in the car."

New tears ran down my face. "I can't. I can't let you do it."

"You think it's up to you?" Daddy got in

the car and slammed the door. He rolled down his window. "You coming?"

I shook my head.

Daddy twisted around to Grace and yelled, "Get those doors closed!"

Grace had barely finished getting both doors closed before Daddy shot back in the drive, pulled out into the road, and screeched away.

I kept talking as if Daddy were still standing there listening to me, and I said what I should have said all along.

"It doesn't matter how many verses you pull out of the Bible, Daddy, 'cause, see, I've seen the chair, I've felt the Lord's presence, and it's good, I know it's a good thing."

And that's when I knew I had to fight him. I had to keep Daddy from hurting that chair.

I took off for the fields, knowing that if I went the shortcut I could beat him to the house. I ran in the tire ruts alongside the rows of corn, and it was like I was just running in place, getting nowhere. The stalks were just a green blur that I caught out of the corner of my eye, as constant as a gnat pestering at my face. I kicked off my sandals, hoping I could run faster, needing to run faster, even though I knew I could beat him to the house. See, I was thinking of Daddy and him splitting up that chair, and this picture came to me of him striking the first blow and a stream of blood flowing out the side of the chair, just like the blood that flowed from the side of Jesus. So I ran faster, not knowing what I was going to do, how I was going to fight Daddy—only knowing that even if I couldn't fight him, if I couldn't win, I needed to be there. I needed to weep at Jesus' feet.

17

I came to the end of the second cornfield and slowed down to a fast walk. I tried to catch my breath, rehearsing in my mind what I was going to say to Daddy. Then, coming out from the fields and looking across the road to the Dabney house, I saw the longest line of cars and trucks and people I'd ever seen in my life. The cars and trucks were parked on the lawn, poked in frontways, sideways, and backways, and then more of them were parked along the road, sometimes side by side, narrowing the road down to one-way traffic.

The people, town folk and strangers alike,

formed a double line along the drive. I could see the Dooleys and the Pettits and the Boles and Old Higgs and Jim Ennis, and beside them Miss Ivy-June. Even from where I was walking along I could hear Miss Ivy-June singing her usual "His Eye Is on the Sparrow," and I saw that she was singing it to some strange man who stood in front of her with a pad and pen in his hands. The man was the shape and size of a Mack truck, which brought to mind Clope Dovey, "The news reporter from the Dothan *Recorder*," as he liked to call himself.

I crossed the street and hid behind Dale Dooley's truck and caught me a better look. Sure enough, that's who it was, Clope Dovey, the reporter with a special gift for insulting everyone he ever wrote about. I knew Daddy would have nothing to say to him. Last time they met was when Clope interviewed him for a special-interest story on "our neighboring towns." He called Daddy's story "The Little Man Who Could" and began by describing Daddy as a chihuahua in Clark Kent glasses. From there it only got worse, and it took Daddy a good couple of weeks to build his pride back up. Since then he's made a second career out of keeping out of the newspapers.

I looked out to the road and saw our car

rolling to a stop beside Miss Tuney Mae's car; then it started up again and turned right into the drive, right into where folks were standing. Daddy had his hand on the horn and was dividing up the line like he was Moses parting the Red Sea. I saw him spring from the car and march around to the trunk. Grace got out and waited by her door, looking like she was ready to jump back in at the slightest need.

I could hear Daddy yelling something about bowing down to a block of wood and what Isaiah had to say about it, and all the usual rumble and noise of the crowd stopped. He poked his key into the lock and looked back up at the people.

"And well you should stand and listen," he said to them. "All through the Bible, all through it, with Moses leading the Israelites out of Egypt, and Noah and his ark, and the prophets Jeremiah and Isaiah, again and again we see the anger and the destruction of the Lord upon those who worship idols and graven images." Daddy held up his hand. "And the Lord said to Moses, 'They are a stiff-necked people. Now leave me alone so that my anger may burn against them and that I may destroy them.'

"Is that what you want? You are violating

the First and Second Commandments of the Lord, and my fear for you is great." Daddy opened the trunk of the car, and I ran out from behind the truck.

"Yes, indeed," Daddy said, "so great is my fear for this town that I . . ."

Daddy stopped in midsentence. He saw me standing in front of him. I moved in closer and said what I had rehearsed.

"I'm going to fight you on this, Daddy— 'cause, see, I've seen that chair and I know it's good." I was breathing hard. My voice was trembling when I spoke but Daddy was listening, looking between me and the folks creeping closer trying to get a better hear of what I was saying; so I talked on. "And these folks"—I gestured to the people behind me— "they've seen, too, and none of your scripturing means anything compared to what they've seen and what they know is true and good."

Daddy wagged his finger at me. "Nothing is good that teaches disobedience," he said. "Nothing is good that turns wife against husband and child against father. Now, you move."

Daddy pushed me aside and turned back to the trunk.

Clope Dovey came up behind him. "Having

a little family squabble, are we, preacher?"

Daddy popped out from under the lid and turned around to see who was talking.

Clope grinned at Daddy and clicked on the little tape recorder he had clipped to his breast pocket.

I saw Daddy shrink back against the car, fumbling behind him to lower the lid of the trunk. I saw his face leaking out blotches of red and his jaw muscles bunching up tight. His eyes had narrowed down to slits, but every bit of the eyeballs showing was focused on that tape recorder. And seeing all this, I knew that Clope Dovey, with his writing pad and tape recorder, had a kind of power over Daddy that no one else had ever had. For the first time in my life, I saw that my daddy was nervous, almost scared, and it made me feel as if something solid and strong inside me had taken a blow, leaving it chipped and brittle.

"Care to give me a bit more of your side of the story?" Clope asked, still grinning and rolling his pen between his fingers.

"No comment," Daddy said, lifting his head a little higher and setting his jaw out like a bulldog.

"Oh, come now, I already heard your sermon here. So what's the deal? You and your daughter having a disagreement?" He laughed. "Don't tell me the preacher's daughter has taken to idol worshiping." He turned to me. "So what's this all about, young lady?"

I heard Daddy clear his throat. I looked at him and he was giving me the eye and then nodding at the trunk. I saw him push down on the lid and heard the lock click back into place, and I felt that same something, already chipped and brittle, crumble inside me.

It hurt my feelings good to think that he believed the only way I wouldn't speak was to show me he wasn't going to chop up the chair.

I turned away from the both of them, feeling that this battle they were having was beyond anything I could handle. Holding back my tears, I stepped around to the other side of the car and joined Grace.

Then Daddy said, in this victorious voice and without looking at us, but keeping his eyes on Clope, "You girls wait here by the car. Don't you go wandering." Then he said to Clope, "Now, if you'll excuse me, I have an appointment."

He marched off, busting between Pete Boles and Miss Ivy-June, startling them good, and then going on inside the house.

I thought Clope Dovey would run on in after him, but he didn't. He came around to where me and Grace were standing, leaned his weight against the car, and turned up the volume on his tape recorder.

18

"Now," Clope said, grinning at us and giving us a close-up view of his crooked gray teeth, "now we got your father out of the way, let's us have a talk. It's about time you young folks had your say, isn't that so?"

He waited, flashing his eyes first at me, then at Grace, then back to me. He waited like we were really going to say something.

"Parents are always thinking they know what's right; believe me, I know. I remember how it is. That's why I always try to give youngsters space in my column. So how 'bout it? How do y'all feel about this Jesus chair?"

He nodded at me. "Go ahead, honey. Speak right up."

I moved around to the other side of the car. Clope Dovey followed me.

"Now, you're a smart girl," he said, hovering over me and breathing burped-up barbecue pork in my face. "Tell me, what were you and your papa discussing?"

"No comment," I said, turning away and looking out to the line of people that had shifted onto the lawn, away from Daddy's car.

He came around and stood in front of me again, switching off his tape recorder. "I'll tell you how it is, honey," he said, leaning forward over me. "I can pretty much guess what was said between the two of you, and you can either verify my hunch or deny it; either way the story goes in. So why not have your say, huh?"

That was it. I had had enough of his Mack-truck looks and his belching barbecue pork in my face and his just-between-you-and-me kind of talk. I was fed up, and when I spoke, all the anger and hurt and worry and hope of the past few days just exploded out of me like the innards blown out of a watermelon.

"No comment!" I shouted. "No comment, no comment, no comment!" Louder and louder I shouted, and the hot tears rolled down my face, making it hard to see the tape recorder I had torn from his breast pocket. I threw it on the ground, still shouting "No comment," and I heard Clope swear at me and felt his hand squeeze around my arm.

"You're going to pay for this, honey pie, believe me."

"I don't think so." Hank Dooley grabbed ahold of one of Clope's elbows and Dale Dooley grabbed the other. Then Old Higgs picked up the tape recorder and slapped it into Clope's big hand.

"You have everything you came with— now git," he said.

Hank and Dale helped him git, and Old Higgs called after him, "An' don't think I won't be calling the *Recorder*. They ain't wanting to be running no snoop paper down there."

Old Higgs turned to me. "Don't be paying him no mind," he said.

I nodded, keeping my head down and watching my tears leave wet circles on my dusty feet.

Old Higgs offered me the gray hankie he'd dug out of his back pocket, and I took it and wiped at my face.

"Miss Tuney Mae's a-calling you." He gestured toward the house with his head, and I turned back and saw her setting in a folding chair under a big beach umbrella.

She signaled for me to come to her, and after getting the nod from Old Higgs, I handed him back his hankie, thanked him, and went to her.

I had to kneel down to see her under the umbrella, and she right away took up my hand and patted it.

"Now, don't you worry," she said. "Your papa's done right, saying what he did about us worshiping the chair. That Clope Dovey can't hurt him. Idol worshiping's dangerous, and it's a preacher's job to try to stop it."

I looked up into her eyes and noticed for the first time that they were blue, like Mama's, only faded like a pair of denims.

"But if you feel that way about it, why are you here?" I asked her.

Miss Tuney Mae rubbed my hand, moving her own hand in circles over it, and she smiled.

"You know me, honey pie. I just love being in the thicka things, and this here is thick, real thick. Just you look at that line an' all those people, all that living going on right there in that line."

I studied the line of folks talking to one another in little clusters, keeping watch on the moving line ahead of them, drinking their soda, and drawing on their cigarettes.

Miss Tuney Mae took her hand from mine and pointed. "Look ayonder at your Sharalee, just joining the line and looking like a spy. Poor child's traded one kind of sneaking for another."

Miss Tuney Mae was laughing, and it didn't seem like she was feeling all too sorry for Sharalee.

"What do you mean by that, her trading sneaking?" I asked, watching Sharalee looking over her shoulder every half second.

"Used to be her sneaking food, an' now she's taking to sneaking over here, knowing her folks don't approve."

"But she's wanting to lose weight. It's for her mama she's doing it," I said.

Miss Tuney Mae shifted in her chair and tilted her umbrella more toward the sun. "I know why she's a-doin' it, an' it ain't for her mama. She may be wanting to lose weight on account of her mama, but she's sneaking on account of herself. Sneaking's her protection. It's the only way she can give her mama what she wants and still hold on to a bit of Sharalee."

"Well, if it works, then . . ."

Miss Tuney Mae nodded. "Oh, it works, but it ain't good for neither one of 'em. That Sharalee will lose the weight, all right, or die trying." She shook her head. "Or die trying, bless her heart."

I didn't like Miss Tuney Mae talking that way. It gave me the shivers, like just her saying that about Sharalee dying would make it come true.

I squinted out across the lawn and searched for something to fasten my sights on and reminded myself that if there was one thing I was learning about Miss Tuney Mae, it was that she loved a good story—and if it wasn't fantastic enough, why then she just added to it till it was.

I saw Miss Anna's pickup bump onto the grass and then stop. Her door opened and she jumped down from the truck and came hurrying toward the crowd. She walked along the line, stopping to chat every now and then, and folks hugged her and patted her back.

"It's a miracle how they found Miss Becky," I said.

Miss Tuney Mae nodded.

"Do you believe in the chair?" I asked her. "Do you believe it was a miracle, her being found?"

Miss Tuney Mae yanked at my arm, pulling me in close to her, and said in this hushed voice, "I know your mama run off."

Her words knocked the breath clear out of me. How could she know? I didn't even know for sure, not really. Anyway, it wasn't true. I looked up into her eyes and I saw her love for me.

"Do you believe in miracles?" I whispered. "Do you believe in the chair?"

"If I'm going to believe in it, then I have to believe in the other, the dark side, Miss Adrienne's last vision. No, I believe in the Lord showing us Himself who He is, each one of us private, an' we don't need to be going to no Jesus chair to get that. We just need to set still a moment an' look inside ourselves."

"But miracles, what about them? What do you believe about them?"

"You wanting me to pray for your mama, honey?"

I nodded. "If you believe."

"Well, all right, then. What you want said?"

I thought on it a good long minute, staring down into Miss Tuney Mae's lap all covered with flower print, and then closed my eyes and said, "Ask the Lord to please send Mama home, and have her very happy to be back, but not 'cause she got hurt or sick or anything, just because, just because, well, she loves us."

I gave Miss Tuney Mae a quick peek, wanting to see if her eyes were laughing or anything, but they weren't, so I went on. "And make Daddy happy and our family happy, and Daddy accepting of the Jesus chair and Adrienne and me. Amen."

Miss Tuney Mae cleared her throat like she was getting ready to say something, but our attention was caught by the commotion going on in the line.

We poked our heads out from under the umbrella and saw Mad Joe, all spruced up and doing this clogging, jigging kind of dancing. Folks in the line were clapping and calling out "Hallelujah" and "Praise the Lord" and "Glory be."

"Well, I'll declare," Miss Tuney Mae said.

Mad Joe was hugging folks and dancing and skipping and doing everything shy of spinning cartwheels. He wove in and out of the line with his hands raised above his head and his face turned up to the sky.

"Another miracle, praise the Lord. Another miracle!" he was shouting. He turned to face the whole line of folks and stood like a preacher calling to his flock. "Brothers and sisters, when you get down on your knees in front of that Jesus chair, sing your praises. Glory hallelujah, sing praises to the Lord. A new miracle, yes sir!"

That stirred folks up good after that. They were all pushing forward, trying to get the line moving faster, and more folks were squeezing onto the porch as if that would hurry things up some. I could see faces mashed up against the screening; and a group of folks, strangers, just outside the entrance to the porch, had fallen to their knees and started their praising and crying and such, right there in the dirt.

Seeing all that made me want to push Miss Tuney Mae's chair into the line and get her praying on Mama coming home right away.

Someone called out, "Only two minutes a person, now, only two minutes up there!" And the word was passed along until it got outside the living room door, where folks were knocking and shouting, "Hey, time's up in there."

Mad Joe was still dancing and, seeing us, he jigged his way over—just to show us his happy face, I guess, 'cause he turned right around again and headed back.

I called out to him. "Mad Joe, what's happened?"

He spun around and jiggitied toward us. He stopped and slapped his hand down on

Miss Tuney Mae's chair and hung over us, panting. Then he pulled a hankie out of his back pocket and wiped his sweating face. He waited until he slowed his breaths down before he spoke.

"Datina's smiling in heaven now, praise the Lord," he said, wiping his face again and laughing his *he-he-he* kind of laugh.

"Are Vonnie and Velita over their spell, then?" I asked.

"Over it and cured, they sure are, and glory hallelujah! And it's just how Datina said. She always said once I believed with all my heart and got straight with the Lord our babies would be cured for sure." He stuffed his hankie back in his pocket and wiped at his face with his free hand. "It was my not believing that held them back—Lordy, it sure was—but no more."

"But how did it happen?" I asked. "They were looking a mite poorly, last I heard."

"And how do you know they're cured and not just having a well spell like they do sometimes?" Miss Tuney Mae added.

Mad Joe nodded at us and stood up straight. "It was me hearing last night how Miss Becky come back. That's when the miracle took up happening."

"But you were wild drunk last night," Miss Tuney Mae said. "You were shooting at my corn."

"Whoeee, I sure was. But, see, that's a part of this here miracle I'm telling you about. There I was out a-roaming the streets and feeling sorry for myself when I seen Miss Becky riding along in the Cobb truck, setting right next to her sister. And they stop and they say how she'd been found at exactly ten o'clock, and how the prayer meeting had broke up at exactly that same time, and how it was a miracle; and hearing it, my own miracle started to happen." He rubbed at his neck. "I'm going to have to write a book about it, I sure am, 'cause all a-sudden I wasn't drunk no more and I was hearing this voice a-telling me, 'Git ye over to the Dabney house and pray, and believeth in what ye ask and pray.' "

Mad Joe wiped at his face again, this time using the sleeve of his shirt. He couldn't keep the sweat from just rolling down his face. Then he said, "Well, I've never been hearing voices before, 'specially not ones speaking 'ye' and 'believeth,' no sir, and I hurried on over here and went on inside, and that's miracle number two."

Me and Miss Tuney Mae looked at each

other, and then I asked, "How was it a miracle, you going inside?"

" 'Cause I heard this morning that the house was all locked up after the prayer meeting for Miss Becky. Locked up till this morning. No one got in last night, 'cepting me. And funny thing, Miss Dabney said she was in that room listening to music and cleaning her art supply stuff most of the night and she never saw me. No sir, never saw me. It was like I was a ghost or something."

I felt these chills on the back of my neck, and my eyes teared up with the wonder of it all.

"Yes sir, the door just opened right up and I went in and I saw the chair and it was glowing this soft blue-white light."

Mad Joe was whispering now.

"So I got right down on my knees and started praying, and then I heard these singing voices coming from every corner of the room. I heard three notes, and they was sung by a angel choir, each note higher than the last, and on the last note it was like something inside me split wide open and came a-pouring out, and when it was through pouring"—Mad Joe raised his voice—"I was clean. I was clean through and through, nary a dark thought left to weigh me down. And that voice said to me, 'Go ye home an' feed your children grain, and sleep believing that they are healed.' And I did. I did just that. And after I fed them oatmeal and slept some, I set out for here to tell the Lord how I believe, and when I come back they were cured—both of them. Both of them cured at the exact same time, not a day or two apart the way it usually is. That's how I'm a-knowing it's forever and it's a miracle, praise the Lord. And I've got me no hangover and I've lost that drinking desire, yes sir, glory be!"

He fell to his knees and held his arms above his head.

"Glory be!" he said again, and then kissed the ground and stood up. He had this big smile on his face and tears in his eyes. "Now wait till that Miz Marshall comes nosying around our place again. Won't she just see what's what! An' your papa, well, maybe this will help him see the light some. He's needing awful bad to see the light."

"My daddy's the preacher," I said, feeling this hurt spot swelling inside me. It was one thing me thinking a bad thought about Daddy, but I wouldn't let anyone else do it, especially someone half-crazy. "He already sees the light," I said. "Shoot, he is the light, and it's just you not believing in preachers that's got you talking that way about my daddy."

"Charity, listen to Mad Joe," said Miss Tuney Mae.

"Listen?" I glared at her. "Shoot, he doesn't even believe in preachers."

"Now, where did you ever get a notion like that?" Mad Joe asked.

I turned back to him. "I've seen the way you don't ever look at him, you look right past him. Always you look right past him like he doesn't exist."

Mad Joe studied his turned-up-at-the-toes shoes and wagged his head. "Miss Charity, I believe in preachers. I do, sure 'nuff. But your papa, he's different. He needs to own people, understand? I can't look him in the eye or he'll own me, way he does this whole town, an' black folks have come too far to let some white man think he can own us. Nobody should own nobody. No sir, he can't own me long as I'm knowing my own mind and looking in my own direction." He stared into my eyes. "Your papa's holding on too tight, you hearing me? He's holding on so tight something's just bound to bust, and when it does, just you watch out, Miss Charity, 'cause all hell's gonna break loose. It sure is. It sure is."

19

Daddy was downright cheerful when he came walking out the front door of Adrienne's house. He was springing up on the balls of his feet and swinging his arms like he had a tune going in his head.

I hurried to the car and climbed in beside Grace and we rode home with Daddy whistling the whole way, and I knew why. He had seen the chair. He had seen the glow. He'd probably talked to it, too. Probably even saw Jesus. He wouldn't say, of course. We never talked about deep-feeling things, but I could tell, and I wanted to throw my arms around his neck, I was so pleased.

That night I had a dream about Mama. I dreamed she had these big green wings attached to her back and she was flying over Casper and bombing it with prunes, and I was swimming after her, trying to take off from the water, but I didn't have any green wings. One of her prunes landed on my head and I started to sink. Mama flew away.

When I woke up my pillow was wet like I had been crying for real. I sat up and wondered about asking Daddy about Mama. He was the only one who really knew if she was coming back, not Grace or Miss Tuney Mae. Daddy knew—and God. I was afraid to ask Daddy about it, but if I could get to that Jesus chair again, why, I could ask Jesus and just wait there till He answered.

I got up and got dressed, thinking all the while about Mama and the day she left. I remembered how after the car rolled out of sight and we'd all gone back inside, there was this funny kind of silence hanging over us. Not the usual kind that hangs around after someone's left, reminding us of that person's voice or laughter or the music that's gone missing. No, this was Mama's silence left behind. The silence she moved and breathed and lived in every day like an extra layer of skin. And when she left, wearing all that green, it was as if she had peeled off that silence and left it here for us, her old discarded skin of silence.

I heard someone banging on our front door.

I went down to answer it but Daddy beat me to it, so I just stayed on the steps watching and listening. It was Mad Joe and he looked a sorry sight. He was holding his hands up like he was praying and they were trembling. The knees of his saggy black pants were shaking, too, and he was saying to the ceiling, "Dear Lord, have mercy, no! My babies. They's cured. You can't take that away. You can't give it, then take it away. No, Lord, You can't give it, then take it away."

"What are you talking about, Joe?" Daddy growled. "What are you doing disturbing us this early in the morning? I've got a sermon to give in a bit, I can't be listening to this. Now, you go on home and sleep it off."

"I ain't drunk." Mad Joe straighted up some. "I come about the Jesus chair. You can't take it, no sir. You got to put it back. You got to put it back now. They's cured. You got to put it back now."

"Now, listen," Daddy said, holding up his hand. "If you want to know about the chair, you come to the service this morning."

"Forcing me to come here a-begging for

my daughters' lives," Mad Joe said, ignoring my daddy. "Yes, sir. I am begging. I have no pride. I'm begging you. Have mercy. Dear Lord, have mercy on my daughters' souls." He dropped to his knees.

"Get up, man. That chair won't save them."

"Please. Just give me the chair. Lord a-mercy, they'll die, don't you understand? They'll die! Give it to me. Give it, I'm begging. I'm begging!"

Mad Joe was crying. Begging and crying and saying how his daughters' blood would be on Daddy's hands. But Daddy stood firm, quoting Scripture, yelling it out over Mad Joe's pleading, and I couldn't stand it. I knew Mad Joe would never get the chair from Daddy.

I brushed past the two of them, with Daddy calling after me wanting to know where I was going, but I just ignored him. I had to get out of the house.

Vonnie and Velita were sitting in the back of their daddy's pickup, parked in our drive, fanning themselves.

"Hey, Vonnie. Hey, Velita," I said, not wanting to be rude but wishing I could run away.

They both looked up at me, and looking back at them it seemed to me the light that used to shine from their eyes had gone. Their eyeballs were dry and funny looking, like those weren't their real eyes atall, like their real eyes were already somewhere else, somewhere the rest of them was wanting to be.

"Vonnie? Y'all all right?"

Vonnie held a bunch of flowers up to her nose and sniffed. Then she said, "Take my body who will, take it I say, it is not me."

I glanced back at the house. I could hear Mad Joe's voice still pleading and Daddy still quoting Scripture.

I couldn't stand it. I ran. I ran as fast as I could away from my daddy. Just like Mama, I was running, trying to block out Mad Joe's voice. Trying to block out Vonnie's and Velita's faces. All their pain and fear was more than a body could handle.

20

The sign pointing the way to the Jesus chair had been pulled out of the ground and was lying facedown in the grass. I ran down the long drive toward the back porch, wondering if the house was locked up again the way Mad Joe said it was the other night. I caught sight of the herb garden sprouting weeds and looking trampled, and I closed my mind to it, not letting the pain reach me, just running on past.

The porch door was open. When I got to the living room door I held my breath and turned the knob. It twisted in my hand and the door opened. I stepped inside. The room was cool and dark. The chair was gone. I called out to Adrienne.

"My God, who is it now?" Adrienne called down from upstairs. "Go away. The chair's not here."

"It's me, Charity."

I heard the clinking of jars and a chair scrape back and then there was Adrienne coming down the stairs. Her hair was up and she had on her painting shirt and her India-print skirt, like the one Sharalee made me.

"Charity?" She gave me this wondering kind of look with her head tilted and her brows furrowed.

I ran to her and threw myself in her arms. "I hate him," I said. "I do. I hate him. I've run away. I'm never going back."

Adrienne grabbed my arms and held me away from her.

"What's happened? Of course you're going back."

"No, never—and anyway, how could you let Daddy take the chair?" I cried.

"Charity!"

"How could you?"

"Very easily. It was a nuisance." She shook her head and her hair fell out of its knot.

"A nuisance! Jesus a nuisance?"

"Charity, calm down. Your father took the chair to the church. Didn't he tell you?"

"But it belongs here. Here's where Jesus is. You saw Him here. We need it. Mad Joe's daughters and Sharalee and the Cobb sisters and—and me! I need it. I hate him! How could he take it? How could you let him?"

"Charity, stop. You know I can't have people in here day and night. I can't. I need space. I need time for my art. I'm not running an amusement park."

"But the chair is helping people—isn't that more important than your art? I—I mean, can't you just wait a bit till things kind of . . ."

"Charity, maybe someday you'll be an artist and you'll understand. Nothing's more important than my art. Nothing. Speaking of which"—Adrienne turned back to the stairs— "I've got work to do." She stood on the first step and looked back at me. "Now you run along, and lock that door behind you."

"No. I'm staying here."

"Charity, please."

"I want to be with you. I want to go to New York. I'm ready. I want to go today."

"Well, I'm not going today."

"But you've got to. I've got to go. I'll never forgive him. I hate him, I really do. Mad Joe's over at the house right now pleading for his girls' lives and Daddy's standing there quoting Scripture. I hate him. He's a liar. He's not like Jesus at all."

Adrienne laughed. "He's a man. He's just human. Really, Charity, if you put someone that high up on a pedestal, they're bound to fall. No one's perfect."

"You are." I rushed up the steps. "You are. You're great. You can stand up to Daddy. You can do anything. Shoot, you can even see Jesus."

Adrienne backed up a few more steps. "Charity, stop. That's just what I'm saying. You can't do that to people, idolize them like that. In the end you just get hurt. You do. Nobody's perfect. Now—now I'm going to go upstairs and get back to my work, and you go on home, where you belong."

"But I don't belong. You even said so, remember? You said I had way too much spirit for a town like Casper. You said you wanted me. You said you would teach me; we'd go to New York."

"Now, wait a minute. I said no such thing. I said that the best art schools are in New York and if you ever wanted to study you should go there. That's all I said. The rest was all in your imagination. My God! I can't even stand my lover living with me full-time—I certainly couldn't put up with an adolescent."

I moved up the steps toward her. "But I can't go back. I can't go home. Let me stay here. I won't even talk to you if you don't want. Just let me stay."

Adrienne moved up the steps and I followed her. She held up her hand. "Stop. Now listen—"

I ran up and threw my arms around her before she had time to say anything more or back away again. I cried full out then and told her she was right about Mama, about her flying the coop. I told her I needed the chair to get Mama back. Adrienne tried to pull away, but I held on. I couldn't help it. It was like she was a window ledge I was hanging on to, to keep from falling. If I let go, I just knew I would die.

I remembered Mad Joe saying how all hell was going to break loose, and that's just what I felt. All hell was breaking loose and I was falling in. I held on even tighter.

"Charity, you're hurting me." Adrienne pushed against me. "You're hurting me, let go!"

She pushed again and I lost the step beneath me and fell, rolling and bumping down to the bottom of the stairs.

I sat up, stunned. Then I felt my neck and my shoulders and decided I was okay. I looked up and saw Adrienne leaning forward over the banister. Her forehead was wrinkled, like she was worried, but she didn't run down to me.

"Are you all right?" she asked.

I rubbed at my sore knees and glared up at her. "No, I'm not, but what do you care? What do you care about people anyway?" I stood up. "Your art! Your art! Big fat deal about your art. Mad Joe and his daughters are much more important, and Sharalee and Boo and Becky Cobb. All of them are more important than some stupid painting, and anyways, excepting for *The Holy*, all your paintings look like a computer could have done them and— and they just leave a body cold all over!"

I felt evil through and through saying that, hurting her, but I wanted to hurt her. I wanted to feel evil.

I waited for Adrienne to cry or something, but she didn't. She laughed.

She threw her head back and laughed, and I ran out of there crying.

21

I didn't go far, just to Adrienne's back porch. I didn't know what to do or where to go. I thought about Mama. Was she still in Nashville? I could go to her. Yes, I thought to myself, I'll find out where she is and I'll go to her.

The porch door slammed open behind me. It sounded like a shotgun going off. I spun around and saw Daddy standing in the doorway.

"I knew you'd be here," he said, glaring at me.

"You took the chair," I said. "You just

snuck over here like some thief and took the chair."

"I did nothing of the kind. Now, I want you home, this instant. I have a sermon to give in a few minutes."

"Well, I don't want to hear it."

Daddy grabbed my arm. "Don't you be sassing your papa." He swung me around toward the exit, letting go of my arm once I was pointed in the right direction, and swatted at my behind. "Now, you git on in that car, this instant!"

I let myself be carried by the swing until he let go of me, and then I caught myself on the threshold and spun back around on him.

"I've already been pushed down a flight of stairs, practically breaking my neck, and now you're yanking on my arm and paddling my bottom. Nobody else better touch me again."

I glared at Daddy and held my hands in tight fists against my sides.

Daddy took a step toward me. "I don't believe you heard what I said. I want you out in that car, now!"

"No, sir!" I backed away from him. "You took that chair, and Mad Joe's needing it. How could you be so cruel? I thought Jesus said for us to love our neighbor. You're always quoting Scripture, Daddy, but never that line. What about loving our neighbor?"

"There is a difference between loving our neighbor and loving Satan, and Satan's in this house. In this very house. You, child, are consorting with the devil, and I will not have it!"

Daddy lunged for me then and grabbed both my arms and started dragging me off the porch.

"No, Daddy. Let go. Let go of me! I hate you."

"If you won't get in the car, I'll put you in the car myself," Daddy said, grunting and struggling to keep ahold of me.

I was wild. I could feel it inside. This wild, evil creature was raging inside of me, and I just let it loose. "No! I hate you. Everyone hates you. Everyone!" I broke free and stood panting in front of the car. "Mama hates you. That's why she's staying away. It's your fault. It's all your fault Mama's gone." I pounded the car and then I ran, and Daddy didn't call me back and he didn't come after me.

22

I didn't know where else to go but to Shara-lee's. They were just setting out for church when I arrived.

"Lordy, Charity, you aren't going to church, even?" Sharalee said when I told her what had happened.

"I don't know who God is anymore, so why bother," I said. "And anyways, I don't want to hear anything my daddy's preaching."

"Law!" was all Sharalee could say.

When they got back from church, Shara-lee and her mama were all full of stories about how Daddy preached a mighty strong sermon on the evils of idolatry and how the church was split right down the middle, with half wanting the chair put back and half wanting it gone. Mad Joe and Old Higgs were leading one side, and Sharalee's mama and papa, and my Daddy, of course, headed up the other.

"Folks are wanting to put it to a vote," Mrs. Marshall said, "but your Daddy said Miss Adrienne's not wanting it in her house anymore, so what's the use of that?"

Mrs. Marshall sat at her kitchen table picking at a sweet roll and looking smug while Sharalee looked on, winding her hair ribbon round and round her wrists.

"I thought they were voting on whether they were going to keep the chair or get rid of it altogether. That's what they wanted," Sharalee said.

Mrs. Marshall shook her head. "But not that Mad Joe. It's over to Miss Adrienne's or nothing. There was just no end to his carrying on." She turned to me. "I told your daddy, Charity, that he'd better lock that chair away good, or that madman'll come and steal it right out of that church. Oh, and I told him you were staying with us, so he wouldn't worry. Most likely he'll be over here to talk to you soon."

I didn't want to see Daddy and I reckon he didn't want to see me, 'cause he never came by, which got Mrs. Marshall talking and digging at me all through dinner. And seeing as how she wouldn't quit till she dragged something juicy out of me, I let out that I had taken a tumble down Adrienne's stairs and that she and I had had a falling out, which set Mrs. Marshall's eyes to dancing, and I could tell she was just itching to get to the phone.

I noticed Sharalee setting across from me looking glum and not hardly touching her dinner. I figured once we got up to her room and closed her door she'd perk up and tell me what was going on, but she just flopped down on her bed and gave me this look like she was wishing I wasn't there.

"I know," I said. "I know you're wanting the chair put back so you can lose your weight."

Sharalee rolled onto her side, facing the wall instead of me. "Sometimes I just hate your daddy," she said. She waited for me to say something, but I didn't know what to say. "I'm sorry, Charity, but really." She rolled back over and sat up, grabbing her pink pillow and hugging it.

Everything in her room was sewn up in

shades of pink. It was like I was sitting inside a strawberry milk shake.

Sharalee sighed and dragged herself over to her bureau. She pulled out two nighties, one for me and one for her. She tossed mine toward her spare bed without even looking to see if it made it.

"Law, Sharalee," I said, picking the gown up off the floor. "I'd think at least you'd be happy to see me."

"Oh yeah, I am, really," she said, her voice as flat as a freshly starched shirt.

"Well, that's a load off my mind," I said, turning my back and slipping on the nightie. I climbed onto the bed.

"No, I am."

"Well, even if we did get the chair back, Adrienne's not wanting it, so what would be the use?" I tucked my feet under her perfectly quilted blanket with the silky pink bows tied between each patch and fluffed up the pillows behind me. I leaned back and all my lumps and bumps and bruises seemed to go soft and melt away.

I watched Sharalee getting into her nightie and when she turned around again to face me, I saw her face was gripped with some kind of worry.

I tried to cheer her up. "Shoot, Sharalee, looks like the weight is just falling off you. I reckon soon enough you'll be skinnier'n me, even."

That seemed to be the right thing to say, 'cause she perked up and came and sat on my bed.

"Yeah, I have lost more. Four pounds total."

"Law, isn't that some kind of record or something, losing so fast like that?"

She shrugged. "Probably most of it's water weight. That's what Mama says."

I looked Sharalee over again, thinking maybe I could tell if it was fat or water she was losing, but I couldn't. All I could see was her eyes all puffy, with blue shadows under them, and seeing them made me feel sad and lonely, like maybe I had lost my old best friend.

"One thing's for certain," she said, "that Jesus chair's sure been working the miracles."

"I reckon."

Sharalee frowned. "What do you mean, you reckon? 'Course it has. Miss Becky's been found, and the Encyclopedia Sisters are cured, I've been losing the weight, and even Boo's got a hair."

"Really?" I hadn't heard about Boo.

Sharalee chuckled. "It's growing out of his shoulder."

"That's not funny, Sharalee. He can't help it he's bald."

"It's true."

"No, you're just saying that. Aren't you? . . . A hair? One single hair sprouting up out of his shoulder? Who wants one there? You're just fooling."

She raised her right hand. "Honest, I'm not. And guess the color."

I shrugged. "Blond, I reckon."

Sharalee laughed her old high-pitched trickling-water laugh and I knew my best friend was back. "It's gray! I swear on a stack of Bibles, it's gray. Now did you ever?"

"I declare, Sharalee, you're putting me on," I said, slapping at her arm and laughing with her. "Who told you this? Miss Tuney Mae?"

"Cross my heart, I saw it with my own eyes. Ask Mama if I didn't."

I wiped at the tears running down my face and tried to stop laughing. "That Boo, I always said he was an old man. Didn't I? Didn't I say?"

Sharalee nodded and wiped at her own tears. "Who knows, fast as that chair's working, he could have a whole garden patch of gray hairs growing out of his shoulder by now."

I rocked with the laughter, and the tears kept coming. Then, before I knew what was happening, I found my laughing tears had turned to crying tears.

"Hey, Charity, what's wrong? What's wrong, honey?" Sharalee inched forward on her quilt and put her arm around me.

I shook my head. "I don't know what's going to happen. I don't know if that Jesus chair's still in one piece. Daddy was so mad about—about stuff and all. And everybody's counting on it, you know? Me praying for Mama to come home soon, and you praying for your miracle weight loss, and Mad Joe— Lordy, Mad Joe praying hardest of all."

"Shh, it's okay. It's okay." Sharalee patted my back. "The twins are already cured, really. I went with Mama to see them the other day and all those sores on their legs were healed and they weren't yella or anything. And don't you worry about me any—I'll lose the weight, I'm real determined. And I bet your mama's turned around and is headed back this-a way right this very minute. Now come on, you're all wore out. You're needing some sleep."

Sharalee set my pillows flat, covered me

over with the sheet, and kissed me good night, and for the first time since Mama had left I felt comforted and safe, and I realized what Mama had meant to me all my growing years.

"Sharalee?" I whispered after she had turned off the light and settled into her own bed.

"Yes?"

"You'll make a great mama someday."

" 'Night, Charity."

" 'Night," I said, and then kept talking. "I know that chair's good. I know Jesus is there. Don't you feel it? Sharalee? Don't you feel Jesus is there when you kneel down and pray?"

"Mm-hmm."

"I don't know. It's like this real holy calm comes over me. Like Jesus is there whispering words into my soul like 'tranquil' and 'fluorescent' and 'silk.' You know? Gentle words. Sharalee? You know?"

I reckon I fell asleep soon after saying that, 'cause it's the last thing I remember thinking about, and the next thing I knew I was listening to some sound coming from far off. I couldn't tell if I was awake or asleep, but the sound was the same each time I heard it. It was a quiet crinkling sound, and I'd hear it for just a second and then it would stop, and then a few seconds later it would come again—*crinkle*—silence—*crinkle*—long silence—*crinkle*. At first I'd hear it, dream a little, then hear it again, but then as I started to become aware of the sound I began to wait for it, and the more I waited the more awake I became, and I realized the sound was coming from somewhere in the room.

I lay there awake with my eyes closed a good while just listening for the sound, and then the sound changed and I started to hear a once-in-a-while *clinking* noise. I opened my eyes and found I was on my left side, facing Sharalee's bed. I strained to see her but the bed was empty. I rolled onto my back and sat up, the quilt still covering my shoulders, and looked out beyond the end of my bed.

"Sharalee!" I called in a loud whisper. "Lord love a duck, what on earth—!"

I leaned over toward the nightstand and switched on the light.

"Charity, what are you doing?" Sharalee whispered back, her mouth full of ice cream. "Turn that thing off before Mama comes in here and fries both our heads in butterfat."

I switched it off, but not before I got a good look at all the goodies piled up around her. Stuff like Moon Pies and Twinkies and cupcakes with two-inch frosting. There seemed to be every kind of cookie set out, too—chocolate chips and coconut shavers and lemon twistees—and then there was the ice cream, which she must have stored in the cooler I saw by her leg.

I crawled to the end of the bed, got down on my stomach, and hung my head over the edge. Sharalee was still eating, and eating fast, even knowing I was looking at her.

"Sharalee?"

She didn't look up from her bowl. She just kept scooping the ice cream into her mouth. "I know this looks bad, but don't worry," she said, talking around her mouthful.

"Don't worry? I'm scared to death! Honest, I am. Sharalee, the miracles are over. Daddy must have destroyed the chair. I didn't tell you about seeing Vonnie and Velita yesterday morning, but they didn't look so cured to me, and they had only just heard about Daddy and the chair. And now you. Sharalee? Are you hearing me?"

Sharalee nodded and grabbed a chocolate chip cookie and crunched it into her ice cream.

I got out of bed and started scooping up some of the junk.

"You've got to stop this. I swanee. In just this one night you're going to put on twice the weight you've lost."

I reached for the box of Moon Pies, and Sharalee's hand came down on my wrist. "Leave it. Just put it all down. Okay?"

"No, this is not okay. Whichever way you look at it, this is not okay."

With her hand still wrapped around my wrist, she twisted at my arm and pulled me down to her so we were face-to-face and I could smell her chocolate breath.

"Leave me alone now, Charity, and go on back to bed." She let go of my arm.

"Sharalee, you're going to make yourself sick eating all this."

Sharalee tore the cellophane off a Moon Pie and stuck half of it in her mouth.

I looked at all the food and reached for one of the lemon twistees. Sharalee slapped my hand.

"I bought all this with my own money at the Food World. You get your own job and buy your own stuff," she mumbled, the crumbs spitting from her mouth and hitting my face.

"Sharalee, I've never seen you like this. Never. Why, you're like a pig. A real pig."

"Shut up! What do you know about it? What do you know about going all day with your mama standing over you watching every bite you shouldn't be eating? What do you know about it?"

I reached for the strands of hair that had fallen in her face and ran them through my fingers. "Nothing. I know nothing about it, 'cepting that you're starving yourself all day and stuffing yourself all night and killing yourself all the time. Sharalee, what are you doing this for?"

"You know."

I hugged her and stood up. Then I climbed back in the bed and said good night.

She didn't answer. I listened to the soft crinkle of another Moon Pie being opened, and I thought about Vonnie and Velita being ready to die but hanging on for their papa's sake, and I wondered if a child ever gets to just please herself.

◈ 23 ◈

Tuesday morning I was sitting alone in the Marshalls' kitchen munching on a mouthful of cereal when Grace came to the door and called through the screen. "Can I come in?" she asked.

I looked around, wondering if it was okay to let someone into a house that wasn't mine. All the Marshalls had gone to work.

I hopped off my stool and set my bowl in the sink. "I'll come out there," I said.

I pushed through the door and Grace slipped her hand in mine easy as you please, like we'd been holding hands all our lives. We sat down on the porch swing hanging from the branch of a tree and started a lazy push, back and forth together, heel-toe, heel-toe.

"I miss you," she said.

"Me?" I was surprised. Grace never seemed to notice I was even around.

"I don't know what to say to the reverend. You were always there. I always talked to you."

"No, you didn't. Grace, you never talk to anybody, just like Mama, 'cepting maybe Boo."

"Well, I miss you."

We sat in silence, listening to the creaking of the swing and closing our eyes to the damp heat settling on our skin.

Grace broke the silence. "I can't see Boo anymore. Can't hardly go out, 'cause Daddy's wanting me close by. He doesn't know I'm here."

"Is he still so angry at me?" I asked, not looking at her.

"He's angry at everybody. Lots of folks come by last night wanting the Jesus chair. Mad Joe come over drunk and saying Vonnie's dying. He tried to break into the church."

I set my feet flat on the ground and stopped the swing. "Do you know what Daddy did with the chair?"

"Yes."

I waited for her to say but she just sat there calm as calm, letting this daddy long-legger crawl up her arm.

"Well, tell me, then."

"It's over to the church. The reverend said Miss Adrienne gave it to him. Said she wanted it out of her house."

I stood up. "I know that, but is it all busted up, or—or what?"

She squinted up at me. "It's still whole. It's locked up. He's holding it till folks come to their senses."

"Poor Mad Joe," I said. I sat back down and we pushed at the ground again. The swing creaked back and forth. I closed my eyes.

"Why's he so mean?" Grace asked, and I knew she was meaning Daddy.

"He didn't used to be, Grace, remember? Remember how he used to take us out for ice cream after Sunday dinner?"

"No."

I opened my eyes. "Well, you were kind of young then, but remember one time in the drugstore in Dothan, when you saw that plastic shovel and pail and you just cried and cried 'cause you just had to have them even though we weren't going to the beach or anything, and Daddy bought them for you? And

213

remember when, just last year, Mama decided to give all her birdcages away at the church picnic, and then when folks were saying they were going to make lamps out of them or use them for real live birds, Mama panicked, and Daddy rescued the birdcages back from everybody? Remember? Remember how Mama just hugged and hugged Daddy?"

"Maybe," Grace said, removing the spider and setting it on the ground. I closed my eyes again, enjoying the floaty way the swing made me feel, and then Grace said, "Boo's got a hair."

I peeked an eye open and looked at Grace. Her face was serious.

"I heard." I closed my eye.

"He's needing the chair back."

"So're a lot of people with worse problems than his."

Grace stopped the swing. "You could get it back."

I laughed and opened my eyes. We looked at each other.

"Of all the people on earth, I'm the least one could get that chair away from Daddy."

"You could, too. You can do anything."

I knew my eyebrows had raised clear up to my hairline. "Since when?"

She shrugged. "Since always, I reckon."

I laughed. "Since never," I said, but for the first time in my life I felt like an older sister. And it hit me, *I'm setting here with my sister. I have a younger sister and here she is and we're talking like real sisters.*

"I can do some things, Grace," I said. "Some real good things, but not everything. Nobody can fix everything." I took her soggy hand in mine and we pushed the swing again, back and forth, together, heel-toe, heel-toe.

24

The next few days were quiet. Too quiet. And it wasn't just that Sharalee and her mama, like most everybody in town, went off to Dothan to work every morning, leaving just kids and farmers and old folks behind. It was the change in the weather, too. The days were dark. The clouds hung lower and lower over the town, still and threatening, like a held breath about to give way, needing to give way, yet holding on a little longer, and a little longer. The heat, thick and suffocating, seeped through the cracks and keyholes of the Marshalls' house, and the central air-conditioning puffed and puffed but couldn't blow it back out.

I spent those dark mornings doing a lot of reading and peering out the window now and then like I was waiting for something: the rain, or Daddy, or Mama—something. And that darkness scared me, being in the daytime and all. It reminded me of the story in the Bible about Jesus and how just before he died—hanging from the cross, nails in his hands and feet, a wound in his side and his head bleeding from the crown of thorns— darkness fell o'er all the land. Every time I looked out the window there it was, the darkness of Calvary.

Friday morning, soon after Sharalee left to put in her three hours bagging groceries at the Food World, and her mama left to cook lunch at the retirement village, and her papa set off for Birmingham, I heard someone's horn honk-honking down the road. I looked out the kitchen window into the gloom, expecting to see a parade, or a wedding party or something.

Instead I saw Mad Joe's truck careen into the drive and flash past the house. He screeched to a stop just beyond the end of the drive and parked under the big shade tree. I saw him stumble out of the truck and figured he was drunk.

He *was* drunk, and one of his daughters was dead. I knew that 'cause he was carrying the stick. It was just like when Granny Slim died and her son, poor as dust, came over to the Marshalls' wanting a pine box to put her in. He brought along a stick, too, pulled out of the woods and broken off till it was just the size of Granny Slim.

I saw Mad Joe do a fast shuffle over to the barn, and I hurried to the door and called out to him.

"He's not here today. He's gone to Birmingham."

Mad Joe turned around, swaying a little as he did, and then when his eyes focused on who I was, he called out, "Help me! Come here an' help me."

I ran out to him and put his arm around my shoulder, thinking he was needing me to help him walk or something.

"No." He pulled away. "I got to leave the measuring stick for my Vonnie."

"Lean it against the barn, then," I said. "I'm sure he'll understand."

Mad Joe turned around again and staggered toward the barn with his hands held out as if he were blind and searching for the way. He set his stick down, but he didn't let go of it. He bowed his head and mumbled something, and then I saw him kiss the stick. When he turned back around he had tears running down his face.

"I'm real sorry, Mad Joe," I said.

He looked up at me and said, "Come on to the truck."

I followed him.

"See." He pointed into the truck bed. "My Velita's dying. We got to save her."

I looked into the truck and saw Velita lying on a mattress and covered up to her chin with a sweat-soaked sheet. Her eyes were closed and she was pale, with sweat beaded up all over her face and her breath coming out in short puffs.

"Lord have mercy," was all I could say.

"Hop in and be wiping her with that sponge." He pointed to a bucket. "We're going t'your daddy."

"Lord have mercy," I said again, climbing into the back and drawing the sponge up out of the water. I sat down and squeezed it out some and then began wiping her face. The truck jerked back and then forward and then back, and we were on our way.

Thirty seconds later we were pulling into my own driveway and Mad Joe hardly took the time to stop the truck before stumbling out, this time with his shotgun in his hands.

I dropped the sponge into the bucket and stood up. "Hey, what are you fixin' to do?"

He pointed the gun at me. "You stay on with my Velita, you hear?"

"But what—"

"You hear? You don't come to the house." He lifted the gun higher.

My legs started to shake so, the whole truck was rocking. I sat back down and nodded.

"You keep sponging. You don't stop sponging."

I nodded again and turned to the bucket. I picked up the sponge and started wiping at Velita's face.

She opened her eyes and stared into my face.

"He's going to kill Daddy," I said. "He's got the shotgun."

Velita licked her lips and mumbled, "He won't do it."

I turned my head to look for Mad Joe and saw him fighting with the shotgun to get through the door.

"He's drunk and he's mad and he's wanting to save you. He'll do it, 'less I stop him."

I made a move to go and Velita's hand came up around my wrist. "Don't let Papa blame himself."

"No, I won't. I got to go."

She pulled on my arm. "Not everyone's meant to live till they're old. That's the natural way of things—God's way."

"Okay." I pulled away from her. She was too weak to hold me. I was climbing out, and she kept talking.

"Tell Papa. Tell Papa it's not his fault."

I hopped down off the truck and ran to the house.

I could hear Daddy quoting Scripture, and talking in his sermon voice, and Mad Joe was shouting over it.

"Who are you? Who are you to do this? My baby's dead! Her blood is on your hands an' I ain't a-leaving without I got the chair. I still got one I can save. I can save her! Now, you move. You move on, 'cause I have no fear of using this."

I ran down the hall screaming. I heard myself screaming. Screaming for Daddy to give him the chair.

Daddy looked up when I came into the

kitchen, but Mad Joe, drunk as he may have been, stayed steady, facing Daddy, with his shotgun not more than a foot away from Daddy's head.

"Charity, it's okay. Now get out. Go on." Daddy's eyes shifted back to the end of the shotgun.

"Give him the chair, Daddy. Lordy, he's going to shoot you! So what if he's idol worshiping. Is it worth your life? Lord a'mighty, is it worth your life?"

"Git back to my Velita, girl." Mad Joe moved the shotgun closer to Daddy's head.

"Daddy?" I pleaded.

"Dying for the Lord's sake is the only way I'm wanting to go, for the way to the kingdom is the way of the cross. Now you go on back to Velita." He gestured with his hands, but he kept his eyes on the gun.

"But what about me? What about our family? If this is what the Lord's wanting, then I don't want Him. I don't want any part of Him. But, Daddy, it isn't! It isn't! We should be living for the Lord, not dying."

Mad Joe backed up, and I thought for a minute he was going to drop the gun. Instead he fixed it so it was set to blast the both of us. "My baby's dying. There's no time. Now, what you say 'bout *your* baby dying for the Lord? What you say now?"

It was only seconds before Daddy spoke, but it felt like forever, waiting to see if he was willing to sacrifice me to the Lord.

He lifted his head, his eyes focused on the ceiling. "Forgive me, Lord, but this I cannot do."

He spoke to Mad Joe. "I'll get you the chair, but when I do, you let Charity go."

Mad Joe waved the gun in our faces. "You get me the chair. You get the chair back to Miss Adrienne's, where it belongs, then we'll talk about mercy."

Daddy walked to the door, followed by me and then Mad Joe and his shotgun. We went up the pathway that led to the church like we were a family going to Sunday worship. Daddy took us through the back way, then into the sanctuary. We walked down the aisle and to the right, to the storage closet. He took his keys out of his pocket, and as he selected the one for the storage door and set it into the keyhole I saw Daddy's hands trembling, and I knew I loved him again, or maybe for the first time.

The procession to the truck was the same as before, with Daddy in the lead, then me, and then Mad Joe, only this time Daddy was carrying the chair.

"You set that in the back with Velita, and, Charity, you ride in there with her," Mad Joe said when we got to the truck. "Baby, your cure is coming, it sure is," he called over our heads with a hopeful voice.

Daddy lifted the chair into the bed and then turned around. He looked at me, and I knew he was signaling something; something was worrying him. Then he grabbed me and shifted me over so he was standing in front of Mad Joe, and he said, "Go on, Charity, climb in back. Hurry now."

I did as he said, and he climbed into the front seat, saying for Mad Joe to get moving.

I didn't understand the change in him until we had gotten under way and I caught a look at Velita. She was dead. Her eyes were open and staring and her face was dry. Even the sheet covering her body was drying out. I drew in my breath and backed off as far from her body as I could get.

By the time we had pulled into Adrienne's drive, I was hunched into a tight ball in the corner of the truck.

Daddy jumped out first and ran around to get me.

"Get out. Come on. Get out and run."

"But when he sees—"

Daddy reached up and grabbed me, pulling me out of the truck while Mad Joe, hoisting up his shotgun, came around to the back.

"Run!" Daddy said, letting go of me. "Run!"

I glanced at Mad Joe catching sight of Velita and I couldn't move. I wanted to. I wanted to run. But I couldn't move.

"Baby! My baby's dead! Lord, Lord, my baby!" Mad Joe wailed. He turned to Daddy with tears streaming down his face. "Move the chair. Move the chair over her body. Go on, move the chair," he shouted at Daddy.

Daddy did as he said.

Mad Joe reached his free arm over the truck and stroked the chair, his eyes shifting from us to the chair and back to us. The shotgun was still aimed at Daddy. "Lord, You can make her live again. You can do it. I believe in Your miracles. I read what You done in the Bible. You raised that widow's son from the dead. Have compassion. Have compassion and do it again."

We all stood there. Watching. Waiting.

"Lord!" Mad Joe's voice shook. "Lord, I believe. Have mercy."

Daddy bowed his head and began mumbling a prayer, and Mad Joe, seeing him, got all fired-up furious.

"You get that chair. Go on. Take it out." He shoved the gun into Daddy's side, making him grunt.

Daddy lifted the chair.

"Now, you take it into the living room and you set it right where it s'posed to go."

Daddy looked at me hard. "Charity, you git. Do as I say!"

"I don't need her, just you now," said Mad Joe, poking the gun into Daddy again and again, forcing him to move forward.

I backed away. My whole body was shaking. Even my breath was coming out of me in trembling fits.

I watched Mad Joe push Daddy along, shouting out the orders, and Daddy marched forward, his voice calling out to the Lord in prayer.

Soon as I saw them turn the corner, heading for the back porch, I ran to the front door, slammed it open, and started screaming for Adrienne.

Adrienne came into the hallway from the kitchen. "Charity, what is it? What's going on?"

"Call the sheriff! Call him! Call him!"

I raced toward the kitchen and Adrienne followed, shouting at me that she didn't have a phone.

I stopped, turned around, and just stared at her, trying to take in what she had said. Then I pushed past her and headed for the living room, not knowing what I was going to do when I got there but knowing that I had to be there.

Just before I got to the entrance, Daddy came through the doorway and closed the door behind him.

"What's happened? What's he doing?" I asked.

"Praying."

"And he's not going to shoot you?"

Daddy shook his head. "It's over. We'll go call the sheriff."

I made a move toward him. I was going to hug him, 'cause it was all over, 'cause he was safe, but then we heard this sound like half the house had just exploded, and me and Daddy and Adrienne, without stopping to think, ran toward the noise still vibrating in our ears. We ran until we caught sight of the blood, Mad Joe's blood, spilling down the side of the chair.

25

Daddy tried to send me away. He called Mrs. Marshall to come get me and keep me at her house, but I wouldn't go, and the more he pushed the more hysterical I became. I wanted to be there. I wanted to see the medics take Velita and Mad Joe away in the ambulance. I wanted to see the sheriff and his people clean up the mess, 'cause I knew otherwise that scene would haunt me the rest of my days. I needed that memory of them setting things right.

I waited with Daddy. We stood outside on the lawn under the black clouds, and I shivered in the heat and humidity as if I were running a fever, and I coughed and my nose ran and my throat hurt as if I had a cold. Daddy rubbed my arms and spoke soothing words to me, but I wouldn't hear them.

They carried Mad Joe out in a body bag, like he was just a sack of garbage needing to be set out by the road. They lowered Velita down off the truck on a stretcher with her own sheet pulled up over her face. They were walking her to the ambulance and I ran out to her before Daddy could hold me back. I walked alongside her and spoke to her, like she could hear me. I needed to believe she could hear me.

"There wasn't time to tell your papa," I said. "But you can tell him. Tell him it wasn't his fault. None of it was his fault."

After the sheriff questioned us and the ambulance rode screaming down the street, Daddy led me through the house to the living room, where a couple of men and a woman were finishing the cleanup. The Jesus chair stood off to the corner with a sheet draped over it as if it were another dead body. I cried as if it were.

I told Daddy I wanted to come home that

night, and we walked back through the fields together, not talking. And the clouds burst open and the rain came down in heavy sheets, and we kept walking, walking slowly through the fields.

26

Soon as we got home, Daddy changed out of his wet clothes, asked if I was going to be all right, and when I said yes, he left and went over to the church. And there's where he stayed. I tried to get him to come on home for supper and then again for bed, but he refused to stop his praying and come out, not even for meals or sleep. Not for anything.

I don't think he thought about how folks would be dropping by all evening, but he should have. In this town, soon as there's word about a death, folks set to baking up goodies and tossing together casseroles to bring to the mourning relatives. Problem was, in this case there weren't any relatives left, so all night long folks were coming to our house in the pouring rain, wanting to know where they should set the food.

I stashed all Mama's kitchen birdcages in cabinets and closets and told folks they could just set their Tupperware down on the counters.

And every one of them had to ask me; they wanted to know what had happened. And I answered the same things over and over and none of it reached me, none of it touched me, I was too numb and too tired. "Yes," I said, "I was there," and "yes, it was just awful," and "No, I'm just fine," and "Thank you for your concern," and "Daddy's over praying at the church." Again and again, the same old thing, "Daddy's over praying at the church."

When Miss Tuney Mae arrived round about ten at night and saw how tired me and Grace were, she patted my arm and nodded, saying how it was best to keep busy.

"That's right," she said. "Just keep moving, don't give yourself any kind of time to think. Just plain wear yourself out with busyness, so when your head hits that pillow at night you'll sleep straight off. 'Cause, honey pie, you don't want to be lying in the dark thinking on this day all over again."

She was right, and when I went up to bed that night I fell right off to sleep—but I couldn't keep myself from dreaming. The dreams were tinted in red, like I was looking at everything through rose-colored glasses, only what I was seeing wasn't rosy. That day, that horrible day, swirled through each scene like a whirlpool that sucked at me, pulling me in, right into its center, and try as I might I could never climb out. I just went round and round, staring into the dead faces of Vonnie and Velita and Mad Joe.

The funeral was set for Monday. I called Thomson's Funeral Home myself Saturday morning, and Mr. Marshall prepared three of the finest coffins he had and took them over to the parlor. Mad Joe and his daughters were going to be buried beside Datina in our grave-yard, and thinking of them resting for all eter-nity just below my bedroom window set my stomach to churning. The grief feeling was starting to flow back in me, and I was prefer-ring the numbness.

I tried again to get Daddy to come back to the house, but he wouldn't even talk to me.

He just kept praying, lying facedown on the floor with his arms stretched out to the sides and his Bible by his head. I left him some of the food folks had brought by and returned to the house to clean up.

I slammed around in the kitchen, putting all the leftovers away and blaming everybody I could think of for the incident—Adrienne, Daddy, Mad Joe, Mama, anybody—so I wouldn't have to stop and think on how much of it was really my fault.

I was wrapping one more pecan pie in Saran Wrap and talking to myself about who was to blame when I heard a knock on the kitchen door. I looked up and saw Adrienne standing there under her umbrella, bouncing up and down on the balls of her feet, waiting to be let in.

I wiped my hands on my shorts and went to open the door for her.

She rushed in and I closed the door behind her, noticing a taxi setting out in our drive.

Adrienne folded her umbrella and took it to the sink. "My God, when it rains in the country, it rains, doesn't it? Everything's turned to mud. I wouldn't be surprised if the whole town didn't slide into the Gulf."

She was talking and shaking her umbrella in the sink while I was looking her over. She was wearing a suit, a tailored suit, with a scarf and a pin and earrings, and her hair all done up and lots of makeup. She looked like a model. She was even wearing shoes, high-heeled shoes.

She stopped her flow of talk and smiled at me. I don't think I smiled back. Her face got all red and she turned toward the sink and her umbrella.

"I've come to say good-bye. I'm going to Paris. I have another show there."

"Oh, it sounds marvelous," I said, and she looked at me like she was trying to see if I was being sarcastic.

I don't know, but maybe I was. 'Cause I was thinking, Why should her life just fall right back into place? How can she breeze in, stir up this whole town, and then just run away to Paris and live happily ever after? It's just like Mama, her running away. Why, she was probably running away from something when she came here. That's what she does. She hides behind her paintings until even they can't block out the trouble, and then instead of facing them, she runs. But what I figure is she'll never know what it's like to stay and fight and to feel the ground always solid beneath her feet. She'll always be running.

When I looked up at her and smiled, I

knew I wasn't mad at her anymore. She was human, just like the rest of us. Just like Daddy and Mama and me.

She smiled back and said, as if she'd read my mind, "I've never been good with people, Charity. I tried to come out from behind my easel, and look what happened. I'll never understand why I was shown those visions. What good did it do?"

"None, I reckon." I picked up the plastic wrap and covered a plate of corn bread. "Seems like being able to see into the future never changed it any. I guess 'cause folks are going to be who they're going to be, no matter what. It's all just bound to happen."

"Then why did I see it? What was the point?" Adrienne stepped away from the sink.

I shrugged. "Maybe there was no point. You just saw it 'cause you were setting still long enough and listening hard enough to see it. Maybe we could all see it if we did that. I don't know."

Adrienne closed her eyes a second and then opened them and looked at me. "I'm going to miss you, Charity."

"Thanks."

She moved toward me, hesitated, and then gave me a kiss on both cheeks, only she missed the second cheek and kissed the air. "Well—uh, good-bye, then."

"Bye."

She took up her umbrella. "Say good-bye to your father for me. Oh!" She reached into the pocket of her suit coat and pulled out a key. "Here's a key to the house . . . My sister's planning on moving down in the fall."

Adrienne saw the look on my face and said, "Don't worry, she's nothing like me, and you'll love her kids."

Adrienne went to the door and when her back was to me and I realized I might never see her again, I said, "I'll miss you, too."

Adrienne gave me a sad smile. "I left you something," she said. "It's over at the house. In the kitchen, with your name on it."

"Thanks," I said, wondering if she could be crazy enough to leave me the chair.

"Well, 'bye." She opened the door and raised her umbrella, clicking it open. "If you're ever in New York . . . ," she called behind her, not looking back.

I stood at the door and watched her climb into the taxi and ride away.

27

Sunday morning I woke from another one of my nightmares. I looked out my window and saw the graveyard below. Three new graves had been dug. I pulled my curtain closed and got out of bed. Keep busy, I told myself. Miss Tuney Mae said to just keep busy. I got dressed for church and knocked on Grace's door and told her to get ready, too. Then I went down the hall to Daddy's bedroom. He wasn't there. I checked his study and then went into the kitchen to prepare him some breakfast. I took it out to the church. He was standing facing the cross hanging on the wall.

I noticed the food I'd left the night before hadn't been touched.

"Daddy, you got to eat. Daddy? . . . I fixed you some bacon and eggs, extra dry, the way you like."

He didn't move. I left the hot food and took away the old.

I went back to the kitchen and cleaned up the dirty dishes. Then I posted a sign on the church door saying there would be no worship service and went away crying, thinking about Mad Joe and how he always loved to make signs.

Grace came down all dressed and ready for church.

"There won't be any church today," I told her.

"Yes, there will. Look out the window yonder."

I went to the window and she was right. Folks were walking right past the sign and on into the church. Me and Grace hurried on over there. As we came through the doors, I looked about me and saw everybody setting where they usually did, and talking just like always. But when they saw us they got real quiet.

I set my umbrella against the wall with all

the others and we started down the aisle, and folks reached out their hands to us, patting us and saying how they were sorry, and how awful it was for me to witness such a thing, and how we were to come on over for some iced tea and cookies real soon. I nodded to them all, Old Higgs, the Boles, and the Pettits and Anna Cobb and Jim Ennis, Boo and his folks, all of them, and then I got to Sharalee. She was setting with her mama and papa and looking like a fashion model with her hair in a swirly bun and a new pink pinstriped dress.

I wanted to talk to her. I had so much to tell her, so much I wanted to say—about Vonnie and Velita, and just remembering them with her, and about the Incident, and how it felt like something good had been cut out of me and wouldn't ever grow back—but I knew it would have to be later.

She winked at me and then her mama stood up, blocking my view of her. "Did you know Miss Adrienne took off? Left yesterday in a huff. Shows what she's made of. But you smile, child. Smile. Look at all the folks standing by your daddy."

I looked, and saw everyone was looking my way, smiling and fanning themselves, nodding at me as I caught their eyes. And then

I looked at Daddy. He was still standing facing the cross, his back to the congregation.

Then I saw Miss Tuney Mae march in with the choir behind her and set herself down at the organ. She started playing the opening hymn and Grace and I moved in next to Mrs. Marshall and grabbed up a hymnal. The rest of the folks stood up to sing, but before we could get a note out Daddy turned around and raised his hands out to us. The music stopped.

"*Suicide*," Daddy said, and then paused, glaring out at all of us. "Suicide is a sin! Let us offer up our prayers in silence."

He knelt down on the floor, fell forward on his chest, and stayed there the rest of the hour. Nobody talked. We all just sat there, and when the hour was up, Miss Tuney Mae played a processional and everybody started going down the aisle, muttering a word or two to Daddy, and then heading back up the aisle and out the door. Finally, everybody had gone. Everybody except me.

I went up the steps and sat down on the carpet next to Daddy. He was chanting or praying or something and didn't even see I was there.

"Daddy, the funeral's tomorrow. You got to get ready."

Daddy raised his head and stared out beyond me, still praying.

"You got to give the service. You got to do a nice job for Mad Joe and his daughters."

He focused his eyes and pulled the Bible to him. "He will burn in hell for his sin," he said, his voice hoarse. He shoved the Bible at me and I knew he was wanting me to read some Scripture, but I didn't. I shoved the Bible back at him and stood up.

"No, I won't read it, Daddy. You said Jesus is inside. You said the kingdom of God is within, and that it isn't a block of wood, or a chair. You said that, Daddy. But I'm thinking you don't really believe it, 'cause your god isn't inside you, it's—it's here!" I picked up his Bible and I slammed it shut and dropped it back on the floor.

Daddy sat up, startled.

"It's true, Daddy. Your god is just words and rules, and—and I don't see how you can believe in the resurrection if Jesus doesn't live beyond that. I mean, isn't that why He rose again? So His spirit could live on inside us? Isn't that what you're always saying, Daddy? Isn't that what you're always preaching?"

Daddy looked up at me, squinting through

his glasses like he was studying me, like he was trying to figure out who I was.

I kept on talking, spitting out everything I had been thinking about the past few days. "Miss Tuney Mae said she believes in the Lord showing us Himself who He is, not just in the Bible but today, right now. And I'm thinking she's right, 'cause I know there's something stronger than those rules inside of me telling me what's good and right, and it's loving people, whatever they do, whoever they are, just like Jesus."

Daddy was getting to his feet and I didn't know if he was wanting to grab me and shake some sense into me or what, so I jumped off the steps and ran down the aisle partways and then turned around.

He was standing in front of his pulpit, his hands gripping the sides, his Bible left behind him on the floor. He started speaking. "Mad Joe . . ."

"Mad Joe!" I jumped in. "You want to know where Mad Joe is? Well, I just bet he's setting in heaven right this very minute, planting him a garden and laughing at us fools. 'Cause, Daddy, God knows. God knows why he did it, and He loves him anyway. That's what I think. God loves us all anyway."

I turned and ran the rest of the way down the aisle, and I heard Daddy say something. It sounded like, "Lord, have mercy," or "A Lord of Mercy," I wasn't sure which, and I was too upset with him to stick around to find out.

28

The sun was shining when I woke up Monday morning, and its warmth and light gave me the courage I needed to go over to Adrienne's house. I wanted to walk through it alone and be with the memories, or the ghosts, or whatever it is the people who take part in the life of a house leave behind. I needed to say goodbye one last time—my way.

I got dressed for the funeral and walked through the fields, letting the mud suck at my sandals. It had a lonely sound, and every once in a while I'd stop and wonder if maybe I should turn back, but I didn't.

When I reached the house I unlocked the front door and stepped into the hallway. I remembered the only other time I had come through the house that way was when Mad Joe had the gun on Daddy. I stood there and remembered, keeping the door open behind me in case I wanted to bolt. And I almost did—the memory was so painful—but then I told myself, No, not this time. I won't run away.

I crept along the hallway and made myself go into the living room. 'Course the first thing I looked for was the Jesus chair, but although everything else was the same as always, the curtains drawn, the fan in the corner, the worn furnishings, it wasn't there, and I wondered again if it was waiting for me in the kitchen with, as Adrienne said, my name on it. The thought gave me the shivers and I decided to march on out to that kitchen and find out. I gave the living room one last glance, letting the memory of Mad Joe and all that blood flash through my mind.

It's okay, I told myself, marching toward the kitchen. It's over. It's all over.

The kitchen didn't look like the same kitchen atall. There were no dishes setting out, or boxes, or sheets; the whole room had been swept clean of Adrienne. It was a kitchen like any other, all except for the painting.

It was her painting, the one she did right after her experiment. I walked up to it and felt that same feeling come over me as the first time I caught sight of it, like my soul had been wiped clear. There was a tag hanging from it. I read it.

"*The Holy:* Dedicated to Charity Pittman, who always looks for the best in people. Charity, this is my best—Adrienne."

I heard a sound behind me and I jumped away from the painting.

It was Daddy. He stood in front of me in his black suit, his right hand smoothing down his hairpiece.

"Hey, Daddy," I said, wondering if he had come to scold me.

Daddy studied my face, saying nothing. Then he shook his head and said, "You're all grown-up."

"Yes, sir."

He frowned. "I'm going to miss you."

I took a step toward him. "I'm right here, Daddy."

He dug both hands into his pockets and studied his polished shoes awhile. Then he said, still studying the shoes, "You know, I've spent the past few days going over the whole summer in my mind, presenting it to the Lord, and the more I saw what I had done, how I had sent a man to burn in hell, the more I felt—well, that I couldn't forgive myself, and I couldn't expect the Lord to, either. I looked everywhere for an answer—a way out. But each answer just seemed to pull the noose of guilt tighter and tighter around my neck. I was trapped. Lord have mercy, I was trapped. The same way I had trapped you and the family, and this whole town, especially Mad Joe. And I couldn't forgive him for setting me on the wrong side of the Lord, for dragging me down in his sin."

Daddy came up to me and rested one hand on the painting and one on my arm. He looked into my eyes. "Then the Lord spoke to me in the voice of a fourteen-year-old girl, and Lord have mercy, I felt His love, His forgiveness."

"Daddy."

He held up his hand. "My sins—" He cleared his throat. "My sins are even greater than you know. I never cared about the chair. I never really wanted it."

"Oh, but you did. You did, Daddy. We were idol worshiping. You wanted to bust it up with the ax. Remember?"

"Because I wanted you. I was losing you, just like I had lost your mama, and I couldn't have it. Now I see—" He paused, and then said, "I want you and Grace to go stay with your mama."

"Stay with her? Isn't she ever coming back?"

Daddy looked back down at his feet. "No, not to stay." He frowned at me, almost like he wanted to cry. "I'm sorry, Charity. I should have told you and Grace sooner."

I nodded. "Yes, sir, you should have. But—well, I think we already knew. I think we knew the day she left. I think all of us knew, we just weren't saying."

He nodded and dug his hands back into his pockets. He started jingling his change. "So," he said, his voice coming out in a whisper, "this God you believe in, you think He's forgiven me?"

"Yes. Yes, Daddy, you taught me that." I reached out to touch him and he grabbed ahold of me and hugged me.

"I don't want to leave here, Daddy," I said, and he squeezed me tight. "I want to see Mama. I want to talk to her lots, but I don't need to leave. Someday I will, maybe, but not now."

"Praise the Lord," he said. "Praise the Lord."

The two of us carried the painting out to Daddy's car setting in the drive. It took a bit of a struggle, but we finally managed to fit it in the trunk. Then Daddy called to Grace and Boo, saying, "Get up out of that dirt, both of you, we've got us a funeral to go to."

Grace and Boo scooped up the weeds they had pulled from the herb garden and tossed them in the rusted-out wheelbarrow Mad Joe had always used. I watched the two of them wheeling the weeds around to the back of the house, struggling to keep the wheelbarrow straight. I shook my head and looked over the roof of the car at Daddy. He was watching them and laughing. It had been a long time since I'd heard him laugh, and it was this *he-he-he* kind of laugh, and it reminded me of Mad Joe.

"You know what I believe, Daddy?" I said.

He turned his head.

"I believe when a body dies, a little piece of his soul lives on in the folks he leaves behind. And, Daddy, I believe there's a little bit of Mad Joe in you."

"Well, that's all right, isn't it?" he asked.

I smiled. "It sure is. It sure is."